Pumpkin Spice & Poltergeist

To us!
To our friendship.
And to the algorithm that knew we
were meant to find each other!

DEAR READER,

Though this cozy romance is light hearted and full of all the fall feels, we'd like to remind you to protect your mental health. Topics within this book include grief, violence, death, ghosts and other supernatural beings, anaphylactic shock/medical emergencies, alcohol, and sexually explicit scenes between two consenting adults.

1

JORDYN

There were many productive, rational ways to use my magic. Summoning the ghost of my ex-girl-friend on the anniversary of our breakup wasn't one of them. Yet here I was, drunk at three a.m. in a circle of salt. Smoke from the dried lavender burning in the bronze ritual bowl swirled around me in misty ribbons. I passed my right hand through them and over the summoning board in front of me.

I stared at my ex's flannel button-down, cleared my mind of any ill intentions or feelings, then spoke her full name to call her to me.

"Louella Samantha Wong. Come here to me."

I squeezed my eyes closed and imagined the last time I'd seen her. What she'd worn. The way her short hair had been effortlessly styled. That coy, knowing smile that had curled the edges of her lips.

"We never got to say goodbye." I held her shirt up to my face and took in the scent that still clung to it. Drunken tears streamed down my cheeks. "I just don't understand what happened. I can't let you go. I can't move on, not until I see you."

The air around me felt like it took a big inhale, and then I heard a fizzle followed by a *pop!*

My eyes flew open and there she was, sitting across from me like not a day had passed. Lou looked exactly as I remembered her: short black hair, warm brown eyes, an open plaid button-down, baggy cargo pants, and shiny black loafers.

Was this the outfit she'd died in?

Had she been relegated to an immortality of wearing the lesbian staple outfit of chunky shoes and cargo pants?

She shifted, and that was when I saw it between the gaps of the button-down: my faded Fleetwood Mac T-shirt. The one she'd *sworn* she hadn't borrowed.

"Did you seriously take my favorite shirt to the afterlife?"

Lou casually leaned back on her arms and gave me an incredulous look. "*That's* what you wanted to ask me?"

"Right. Sorry, Lou," I said sheepishly. "That's not why I'm here."

"This is such a *you* thing to do, Jordyn," she said in her normal bored, monosyllabic tone. "Why exactly did you disturb my eternal rest? Needed a ghost's help picking an outfit?"

I was suddenly very aware of my cuticles and that the reason I'd called her to the land of the living was too embarrassing to admit out loud.

"So . . . how's the afterlife treating you?" I asked, adjusting my wire-rimmed glasses. "What's it like?"

Lou shot me a sideways glance. "You know I can't tell you that. There are rules. Even if I wanted to tell you, my spirit wouldn't be able to speak the words." She zipped her lips and threw away the imaginary key.

She'd always been playful, but there was something freer about her spirit. I'd half expected her to yell at me when she appeared. We didn't exactly end things on good terms . . . which had been my fault.

"I thought you'd be a little more vengeful and less, uh, mellow." I toyed with a strand of my long chestnut-brown hair. "You're not mad at me?"

She cocked her head and watched me closely. "For summoning me or breaking up with me?"

"Breaking up with you."

"I was." Lou rolled her eyes. "When I was alive, I was very mad at you for breaking up with me for absolutely no reason other than you were scared of your own damn feelings. But I'm over it now. I don't have those sorts of worries now that I'm dead."

"You sound a little mad."

She crossed her arms. "I'm not mad!"

The floor trembled, and I heard the distinct sound of spell jars rattling on the shelf behind me.

"The shouting isn't helping the whole 'not mad' thing."

"Fine!" she blustered, throwing her hands up like she used to when we fought. "Did you summon me to be an angry spirit or something? Would smashing mirrors and possessing bodies make you feel better about yourself, Jordyn?"

The more she raised her voice, the more present she felt. It was as if she were shifting from ether to flesh and bone.

"Shh!" I held up a hand to quiet her. "You're going to wake Iris!"

"You're still rooming with her?" Lou looked around and shook her head in disappointment.

3

Iris and I shared the two-bedroom apartment above the Poisoned Apple Apothecary and ran the shop on behalf of the coven. I'd moved in with my fellow coven member and best friend a few years ago, before Lou and I'd gotten together officially. It was hard to imagine living with anyone else now. Who else would put up with me?

"Am I here so you can hash this out *again*?" Lou asked, pulling my focus back to her as she eyed the inner circle of salt. "You want to justify to me why you tucked tail and ran?"

I frowned down at the empty bottle of red wine beside me. I wished I had more, but if I left the summoning circle, Lou might be gone by the time I returned. I wiped the fresh bout of sloppy tears from my eyes. I should've just watched a Jane Austen movie and cried over a bowl of ice cream like a normal person! This whole closure thing was a mistake.

"I'm sorry, Lou. I just missed you and wanted to say goodbye. . . and that I'm sorry for everything. Truly."

Lou softened a little at that. She'd always given me way too much leeway when it came to romantic responsibility. "This is the gayest thing we've ever done, by the way," she said. "Summoning me from the afterlife to have one more long talk about our feelings."

We both let out a little laugh, and the tension between us simmered into silence for a moment.

"How did I die?" she asked as if she wanted me to tell her a bedtime story.

I blinked at her. "You don't remember?"

She pursed her lips and shook her head. "I only remember flashes of that day. Brunch, maybe? But then nothing. Only peace . . . well, until now."

I looked up at her, my wet eyelashes clumping along my bottom lids. "Car accident. But something about it just never made sense. They said your car reeked of alcohol." I wiped my nose with the back of my hand. "I told them you stopped drinking years ago, but they wouldn't listen. They found your car in a ditch at the turnoff to Maple Hollow."

Lou's brows knitted together. I longed to smooth that divot between them with my thumb like I used to, but I knew my hand would just pass straight through her. "Was I coming back to see you?"

"Were you?" I asked, unsure of which answer would be worse.

"I don't know." She shrugged. "Guess we'll never truly know. It's okay, Jords. I've moved on. I think it's time you did the same."

"I know." My voice wobbled. "I just wanted a chance to apologize. You can go back to eternally resting or whatever it is you're doing on the other side."

Lou's cheek dimpled on one side. "Don't make the same mistakes with the next girl, okay?"

"I won't. I promise." I sniffed and wiped my nose again. "Goodbye, Lou."

Lou hugged her knees to her chest and gave me a nod. "Goodbye, Jordyn."

I swept my hand across the salt, breaking the circle and releasing Lou back to the afterlife. I waited for her corporeal form to fizzle away like the other spirits I'd summoned . . . but she didn't.

One of Lou's closed eyes peeked open, then the other.

Her frown lines deepened as she looked at me. "What did you do?"

"I . . ." I looked around the room, then down at my spell book, examining the summoning circle. Nothing was amiss. "Nothing. It was just a normal summoning."

Lou narrowed her eyes. "What did you say when you summoned me?"

"'We never got to say goodbye,'" I repeated, trying to remember the exact phrasing. "I can't move on until I see you?"

I went over what I'd done before she'd appeared. I'd performed the ritual in the exact same way I'd always performed it. I hadn't even dipped into my black magic stores to ensure she'd be more visible.

"Oh, boy." Lou let out a long-suffering sigh. "That explains it."

"What?" My eyes flared wide. "What did I do?"

"I had this weird feeling, like a hook in my gut." She patted her stomach. "Like I was here for a reason."

"What reason?"

"Just like you said." Lou looked me over, arching one slender brow. "I'm here to help *you* move on."

"What?" I spluttered, knocking over the wine bottle and bolting to a stand. "That's not what I meant at all. I take it back!"

Lou stood too, walking straight through my armchair and toward the window like the phantom she was. She folded her arms and grinned at me in that delightfully mischievous way of hers. "I'm going to help you find a date, Jordyn. And I'm not going to let you mess it up like you did with me."

"Oh no. *Nope*." I popped my P. "Absolutely not."

I dropped to my spell book and rapidly flipped through the pages, trying to find a way to send her back. I was *not* going to consent to the ghost of my ex-girlfriend playing matchmaker like some reality TV host. I thumbed through page after page, but the right spell didn't catch my eye.

Lou's loafer kicked the book out of my hands.

"What the hell, Lou! You can touch things?" My eyebrows shot up. "How did you master that so quickly?"

The only spirits I knew who would purposefully move solid objects had spent years stewing in their rage. Lou wasn't a vengeful spirit and had only been gone a relatively short amount of time.

"You summoned me here to help you, whether you meant to or not." She bounced on the balls of her feet and smiled again. "And I can't leave until I fulfill that wish."

"I made no wish!"

"You did."

"No, no, no." My eyes frantically searched the room. "I just wanted to clear the air, not have you become some fucked-up otherworldly dating service!"

Her grin turned foxlike as she looked me over. "This is going to be fun."

2

HARLOW

I stared up at the swinging burgundy sign emblazoned with an orange maple leaf and a black witch's hat. Shimmering golden lettering over the top read Witch's Brew Café.

"Well, this must be the place," I mumbled to myself.

Shifting my backpack strap on my shoulders, I took in my older sister's café. It was impressive, larger than I thought it would be, with grand bay windows that looked out over the town square. She'd owned the place for years and yet this was the first time I'd seen it for myself.

Like everything in Maple Hollow, the café had kept with the spooky, autumnal colors of black, orange, burgundy, and gold.

The town apparently swelled with tourists in the fall and boomed in the weeks leading up to the Halloween Festival. But Maple Hollow and its townspeople were clearly committed to the bit year-round, given there was a dried-flower florist, an old-timey candy shoppe, an apothecary, *and* a vintage bookstore all circling the town square, in the middle of which stood a black gazebo surrounded by crooked trees.

Part of me wanted to wander around, but there would be plenty of time for me to explore the kitschy little town after I settled in.

The café door chimed as it opened.

"Harlow!" Willow called while she ran toward me, dusting her hands down her mustard-colored apron.

I ran forward and wrapped my sister in a big hug. "Hey, Wills."

"Come on in," Willow said, ushering me through the door. "I've just closed up shop for the night, but I've got a few cinnamon rolls left over. You want a coffee? Or a tea? How about a chai?"

I noted the time, just after six. I'd been traveling all day and with the sun setting over an hour ago, I was ready to fall into whatever bed Willow had waiting for me.

"Peppermint tea would be perfect, thanks." I hung my backpack on the coatrack made of gnarled broomsticks by the door. "This place is incredible," I said, taking in the space. "The whole town is like something out of a fall fever dream."

Booths ran along the wall to the right. Cushy armchairs and low tables dotted the rest of the space, making it seem like a cozy place to read on a gloomy fall evening.

"It's a little eccentric." Willow laughed as she pulled out a plate and used a set of long tongs to grab a cinnamon roll from the cabinet.

"Just a little." I shifted my weight as I lingered in the doorway.

"Sit," Willow instructed, nodding at a stool by the bar.

"Right." I dropped onto the stool across from her and twiddled my thumbs. "Thanks for letting me stay here with you," I added, trying to break the ice. "I know we haven't really caught up in a long time—which is totally my fault, by the way—but I really, really didn't want to have to move back in with Mom and Dad."

Willow let out a soft laugh and shook her head. "I don't blame you." She poured some hot water into a candy apple-colored teapot and slid it over to me along with a matching cup and saucer. "I'm glad you're here. I could use the help around this time of year, so it works out for both of us."

"Thanks." I knew she was just saying it to make me feel less pathetic. "I promise I won't mess this up." I didn't know if I said it more for her or me.

Willow leaned her elbows on the counter, and I took my sister in. She was four years older than me, and while we'd been close as kids, we'd grown apart after I'd moved away from home. I thanked my ADHD and my proclivity to forget everyone who wasn't directly in front of my face. I always intended to call, but it got harder and harder over time. And when you were constantly fucking up and switching jobs, you really didn't want to call your big sister and tell her about your latest failures. After my most recent bout of hyperfocus—this time on opening an online T-shirt store out of a studio apartment in Boston—had gone bust, I'd been left with two digits in my bank account and nowhere to go. That was when I'd called Willow.

I took a bite of the cinnamon roll. The delicious flavor of spicy cinnamon and nutmeg blended perfectly with the sweetness of the icing sugar that melted in my mouth. "This might be the best thing I've ever eaten," I said, my chipmunk cheeks full as I took another giant bite.

"Wyatt," Willow said, her face tingeing rose. "He's our local baker. I get all of the cabinet food from him."

I eyed my sister. "Marry him."

She rolled her eyes at me as I waggled my eyebrows at her. It might have been years since we'd seen each other, but I still knew my sister.

Instead of replying, she reached across the bar and touched a strand of my white-blonde shag haircut. "I like the 'do. Very eighties rockstar."

"Thanks." I smiled at her. "You, as always, look way too cute."

My sister had golden-blonde hair, deep blue eyes, and freckles across the bridge of her nose. She had a warm countenance that I was sure made her the perfect cozy café owner, always ready with a cup of coffee and an easy smile.

"Well, you must be exhausted from the bus ride here," she said, not taking the compliment. "I've got the guest room behind the kitchen all ready for you." She waved behind her. "My apartment is just up the stairs. I'll give you the tour later."

I looked around her to the back door and the light coming from her staircase just off to the right.

"But, um, do me a favor? Don't go exploring the town until tomorrow. There are some things I need to tell you about this place first."

"I'm not going to get abducted by a vampire or something, am I?"

She guffawed, her eyes flying a little too wide. "We'll just, uh, talk in the morning, okay?"

"Well, *that's* not ominous," I said, taking a sip of minty tea. "Why don't you just tell me whatever you're going to tell me now? I'm not going to be able to sleep with that sketchy warning of yours."

"You're perfectly safe here," she assured me. "You're with me. The locals will leave you alone."

I frowned at her. "And why wouldn't they leave me alone?"

"Okay, fine." She threw up her hands in mock frustration. "You always do this."

"You always taunt me!" I shot back.

Willow leaned back against the countertop. "If you were a tourist just passing through, I'd never admit this to you, but since you'll be staying here for who knows how long, you should know the truth. There's more to Maple Hollow than meets the eye."

"You mean besides the way you're all obsessed with Halloween and pretending to be witches and vampires and things?"

"Yeah," she hedged.

I watched her worry her lip for a moment before she got on with it. Her persistent need to shield me from the evils in the world was an old habit. Something only an older sister could get away with.

"See, the thing is, this town . . . Maple Hollow . . . is . . . *special*," she said. "They're not pretending. Magic is real, and a lot of magical creatures live here."

I swallowed a big gulp of tea that painfully stretched my esophagus all the way down. "I'm sorry. I think I just had a stroke. What did you just say?"

"They're drawn to the haunted wood," she said. "It pulls on all things paranormal."

I started searching around the room for hidden cameras. Had my sister suddenly developed a penchant for practical jokes? "You're saying this town is like the Hellmouth in *Buffy*?"

"Kind of." She scrunched her face as she teetered her hand back and forth in a so-so motion. "It's a gathering place for paranormal beings: witches, werewolves, monsters, vampires, demons—"

"Aren't demons and vampires the same thing?"

Willow shook her head. "Common misconception. Demons give off more finance-bro vibes. Vampires give off more Victorian-royalty-who-wants-to-drink-your-blood vibes." She cringed. "You'll know them when you serve them."

"When I *serve* them?" I practically bolted out of my chair. "They all come in here for scones and pumpkin-spice lattes? Willow, what the fuck is wrong with you?"

She held up placating hands. "See, *this* is why I didn't want to tell you until morning."

"So I can't go for a walk without being eaten by a monster?"

"No one here is going to eat you. Don't be so dramatic."

"You just told me vampires are real! I think I'm entitled to be a little dramatic!" I turned in a circle, the café's dark windowpanes staring at me like empty eye sockets. I wondered if a beast was watching me from the shadows.

Willow waved a hand in front of my face. "What are you looking at?"

"I'm wondering if a pack of werewolves is waiting to hunt me down," I muttered.

"There's nothing lurking in the darkness," Willow said, coming around the counter to my side. "Well, nothing that wants to hurt you, at least," she amended, which did nothing to comfort me. "And maybe don't go walking through the graveyard alone, or the orchard, or generally anywhere that's shrouded in mist . . ."

"Wonderful," I said tightly.

"Now you know why I was so hesitant to say yes to this."

She gently squeezed my shoulder. "Are you sure you don't want to just move back in with Mom and Dad?"

I shook off her hand and straightened my shoulders. That was a million percent *not* an option. I would rather grapple with the paranormal than deal with our parents' passive-aggressive judgment. The image of Mom's eye rolls and Dad's pointed jibes made me clench my jaw. I strode to the rack of witch's brooms and grabbed my backpack.

I gave one last glance toward the shadowed town square. "I can handle a few demons over Mom and Dad any day."

Willow smiled, and a twinge of mischief twinkled in her eyes. "You'll fit right in."

3
JORDYN

I turned off the light and lay in bed, staring wide-eyed at the ceiling for several minutes before turning the light back on, only to find Lou sat atop my dresser, chin in hand, watching me.

I glared at her. "You're seriously watching me sleep?"

"You're the one who summoned me, okay? And on the one-year anniversary of our breakup too," she said with a shake of her head. "That's really lame, Jords."

"Stop calling me that," I pleaded.

I'd never liked the nickname. It sounded too much like the portmanteau for jean shorts, which I'd never be caught dead in—no pun intended.

Lou surveyed the room with a tired expression. "I missed this place. It looks exactly the same. Like a moment frozen in time."

"It's only been a year," I countered.

She shrugged. "Time works differently once you die."

To be honest, I wasn't sure I wanted to know little facts like that about death. It made my stomach sour to think about it for too long. But there was something I was still curious about when it came to Lou's passing.

"Do you really not remember it?" I asked a little more softly. "Dying?"

Lou's lips curved downward. "I don't remember any of it. I don't remember that day at all."

I sat straight up and brought my knees to my chest to hug for comfort. "You don't remember where you were driving when you died?"

"Nope." She raised a transparent shoulder.

The knot in my gut eased a little. I had long suspected she'd returned to town to see me, but I didn't have the confidence to ask if I'd been the reason . . . and if she didn't remember her death, I wasn't about to dredge it up. For a ghost, she actually seemed quite chill about the whole thing.

Lou frowned at the gift basket she was sitting next to. I hadn't dug into it yet. "Who sends fish in a care package? That swamp monster's still obsessed with you, huh?"

I rolled my eyes. "Juniper is harmless."

Lou's prying gaze continued to scan the room, and then she screwed up her face as if she were focusing hard. Her hand sank through the wood of the dresser and into the top drawer. "Got any new toys since last I was here?"

I made an embarrassed squeak. "Get out of there!"

She pulled her hand out and giggled. The sound made a hundred memories of her laughter fill my brain all at once, but the one of us at the Halloween Festival shoved its way front and center. We'd drunk spiked cider until we'd been tipsy then soaked up the booze with two funnel cakes each. No surprise that we'd thrown up several times on the walk back to my place.

"Don't be like that." She wiggled her brow. "We had a lot of fun with Mr. Buzz-Buzz."

"For real, Lou, go away." I groaned. I threw my pillow at her, but it just flew straight through her and clattered into the jewelry box on my dresser.

She ignored me and peered into the drawer that had shimmied open by the force of my attempted pillow assault. "A remote-controlled one? Fun!"

"Oh my god. Please." I hid my face in my comforter, my words coming out all muffled when I added, "Can't you at least just go to another room while I'm sleeping?"

Lou sighed. "Fine." She hopped off the dresser and landed without a sound on wooden floorboards that should've creaked. "Maybe I'll go tidy up the apothecary shelves. You always leave them a mess. Or maybe I'll go wander around town, do some snooping."

"Whatever floats your boat," I mumbled. "Thank you."

"You've got to get some rest anyway," she said. I peeked up from the covers and watched Lou thrust her hands into her pockets and rock back on her heels. "Once we get that stick out of your ass, we are going to find you a new girlfriend. Not as amazing as me, but let's be real, no one could be."

"Still so humble." I lifted my head fully and narrowed my eyes. "That is not happening, by the way. I don't have time to date right now. And it's none of your business, remember?"

"Oh, but it is," she said with a wicked grin. "Unless you want me hanging around for the rest of your life. And don't for a second think I won't be watching you use that remote-controlled doodad."

"I can't believe this is happening."

Maybe going on an actual date wouldn't be such a bad

19

thing. A year *was* a long time to be dating only the toys in my top drawer . . .

One date and then Lou could go back to wherever she'd come from.

"That's what you get for disturbing my eternal rest without clear intentions. Think of it as a learning experience and a ghostly dating service."

"I'm sorry, okay? For all of it."

She gave me a broad smile. "I'm not."

A knot caught in my throat at the unexpected care in her words. I tried to return her smile, but the pang of grief in my chest returned. It was an odd feeling to miss someone who was right in front of you.

Well, sort of.

4
HARLOW

Willow woke me up at the ungodly hour of five fucking a.m. the next morning—no wonder she went to bed so damn early. I begged for another hour of sleep, but she insisted that I needed to be up, dressed, and caffeinated before the rush of morning customers. The only silver lining? I was too exhausted to question the patrons who came into the café.

"I'm surprised vampires and demons are early birds," I whispered to my sister as I refilled the napkin dispensers.

"They come in later," she said, as if that were common knowledge. "And no paranormal talk in front of mixed company." She nodded to a family in a corner booth who looked like they'd walked out of the pages of an *L.L.Bean* catalog. All that was missing was a white picket fence and a yellow lab. "If anyone asks you about it, you start with 'legend has it' before you say anything, got it?"

"If you keep waking me up at five a.m., legend has it you won't have to worry about me speaking to anyone," I muttered.

"Muffins are here!" a man called victoriously from the hall as he came in from the back door. He carried giant white boxes stacked five tall and used his knee to swing open the half door to behind the counter.

"Our hero!" Willow exclaimed in a fake Southern belle accent. "We were just about to run out."

The man's gaze slid from Willow to me, and he inspected my apron with a questioning look. "Who's the new recruit?"

"This is my little sister, Harlow," Willow answered him then pointed her chin up to the box-toting guy. "Harlow, this is the local baker, Wyatt."

I scrutinized him more, realizing his eyes were a little too golden to be human. His dusty-brown hair curled at the ends and fell into his eyes, and his canines were slightly elongated. There was something decidedly lupine about him that I wouldn't have picked up on if my sister hadn't told me. I would've just thought he was a handsome man and left it at that.

I must've been studying him a little too long because Willow leaned into Wyatt and whispered, "She knows."

He inclined his head. "Ah." He flashed me a wolfish grin. "You must be freaking out, huh?"

"Just a tiny bit," I squeaked with a forced smile.

He playfully ruffled Willow's hair, tousling strands out of her messy bun. "Took this one weeks just to look me in the eye. You're already way ahead of the game."

I darted a look at my sister at the casual display of affection. Her smile fell into something more pointed, and I knew she was telepathically saying, *Don't you fucking dare*, which made me want to make a witty remark even more. But I resisted. She'd taken me in and given me a job. I couldn't be a total asshat to her on the first day. . . even though it was obvious the werewolf had heart eyes for her.

Instead, I turned to Wyatt. "I'm surprised you're up so early. I would've thought people like you were night owls."

His smile was charming and slow, and I began to wonder if he changed into a golden retriever instead of a wolf. "I am a night owl. I'm just about to hit the hay, actually."

"Oh, right." I bobbed my chin. "Makes sense."

"This is my last delivery of the morning," he said. "Sorry it was a little late today. Midnight Market's order was 'not to their satisfaction.'"

Willow rolled her eyes. "Oh, Billy."

"Last week, he said the scones were overdone," Wyatt said, "even though they sold out by the end of the day. This week, he said they were undercooked. There's no winning with him."

"Visitors rave about your scones." Willow placed a hand on Wyatt's forearm but instantly removed it when she spied the smug smile on my face.

"Well, except for the smoked mackerel and Muenster scones I tested out a couple years ago." His nose scrunched up like he was still haunted by the smell.

"Katie is persistent." Willow turned to me. "She's a local fishmonger—a sweetheart but has an odd obsession with putting fish in everything. You'd think she'd be sick of the stuff by now."

"In her defense, she's found her calling. I admire anyone who sees what they want and goes for it." The gleam in Wyatt's eyes turned into a lustful blaze when he looked at Willow again.

My sister's cheeks flushed. "Anyway"—she cleared her

throat—"I should get back to it before the midmorning rush."

"Right, I'll see you tomorrow." Wyatt gave her a salute before heading toward the back door. "Nice meeting you, Harlow."

"You too," I said, bouncing on my toes as I waved. I looked at my sister. "I don't have much to base this off of, but he is the nicest werewolf I have ever met."

She snorted. "He's something special, it's true." I opened my mouth to say more, and she held up a finger at me. "Don't!"

An elderly woman toddled up to the counter and ordered a pumpkin-spice mocha. Willow gave the woman a warm smile and began to write the order on the side of a to-go cup before she paused like something had just dawned on her.

"Oh shoot." Willow looked at me. "We're out of cloves."

The woman watched with a question on her brows as her eyes pinged between my sister and me, her coin purse still clutched in her wrinkled fingers.

"That's a shame. I've heard it's the best pumpkin-spice mocha for miles." Her granny-like voice was full of defeat.

Willow opened the register and fished out a crisp twenty. "No worries, we can fix that in a jiffy." She looked between the elderly lady and me. "Maybe I should go."

My confusion marked my face. "I can run an errand for you. Just tell me where to go."

"I know. I just . . ."

My frown deepened. Did my sister really think I couldn't run to the supermarket and buy cloves for her? Was I really so pathetically bad at things that she didn't trust me with this?

I nudged her with my elbow. "Wills, come on."

"Okay," she relented. She feigned a smile at her customer, who was watching our exchange as if we were on some early morning talk show.

"Go to the apothecary down the street and ask for ground cloves. Fresh. Tell them it's for Witch's Brew."

"Apothecary?" I asked incredulously. "Should I bring a wicker basket and don a cloak?"

"Only if you want to be mocked mercilessly." Willow snickered, waving the twenty-dollar bill at me. She tipped her head to the front door. "It's five buildings down. Can't miss it."

I grabbed the twenty and tucked it into my pocket, then leaned toward Willow to whisper, "If I'm not back in ten minutes, give your boy toy my jacket to sniff so he can track me down."

"I knew having you move in with me would be fun," Willow said tightly, nostrils flaring as she shoved me toward the door.

5

JORDYN

"I'm here! What is it? What's the emergency?" Iris rushed into the apothecary. The autumn breeze made her hair dance in long red waves as the door behind her slowly closed.

When I'd rapped on her door this morning and asked her to grab "the big book," she'd bolted off to get it without another word. Now, she hefted her great-great-grandmother's grimoire onto the countertop with a heavy thunk. A basket of vials clinked as she flipped open the black leather cover and looked up at me with curious green eyes. "What's going on? I expected you to have lost a limb or something. What's wrong?"

This was why Iris was my best friend. She always showed up for me, no questions asked.

I pointed at Lou, who was standing in front of the bundles of dried herbs on the long wooden table in the middle of the store. "That's my problem!"

Iris's brows pinched together. "You needed the heavy-duty magic to help sort the herbs?"

I glared at Lou. "She can't see you, can she?"

"Nope," Lou said with a shrug. She looked entirely too smug.

"Who are you talking to?" Iris demanded. "Have you partaken of the mushrooms again? Those are for customers, Jordyn."

I leaned against the counter and rubbed my temples. Even my patented hangover elixir wasn't working today. Not with Lou's ghost looming like the smuggest apparition in the world.

"I summoned a spirit last night," I admitted.

Ugh. Is this my punishment for breaking up with her? Karma is a bitch.

"What, nothing good on Netflix?" Iris taunted.

Summoning a spirit wasn't entirely uncommon for witches. She and I used to do it all the time when we'd been bored teenagers.

"This one is sticking around." I wrung my hands as I glanced at Lou, who was crouched by the front door, giving belly scratches to the shop cat, Ichabod.

Iris followed my line of sight. "Is the spirit here with us right now?"

I nodded. "Lou, why don't you pick something up? Levitate something." I waved to the vials beside her. "Come on, help me out here."

"Lou!" Iris exclaimed. "You summoned the ghost of your ex-girlfriend?"

"Oh, she's mad." Lou chuckled. "Madder than even me."

"I can't think when the two of you are talking at the same time." I pointed at Lou. "You, be quiet." I turned back to Iris. "It was the one-year anniversary of our breakup and I was drunk and I never got to say goodbye to her and I just thought—"

"You 'just thought'?" Iris groaned. "You 'just thought' you'd bring her earthside for a little walk down memory lane?"

"Something like that," I said, feeling pathetic. "And now she won't leave."

Iris started flipping through the withered pages in front of her. "Typical! I told you to let it go. Let sleeping dogs lie. But no! You had to be a clever little witch, and now you've got a *poltergeist* on your hands. Delightful!"

"She's not a poltergeist—"

"Not yet!"

"I just wanted to say goodbye!" I shouted back.

"Of course you did, you—"

A glass vial shattered on the floor, interrupting Iris's reply. I glared at Lou, who just winked at me in response.

"You're worse than the cat," I spat, waving to Ichabod, who was lying in a sunbeam.

"It really is Lou, isn't it?" Iris asked, her voice dropping to a whisper. "Holy shit."

"I can't get rid of her."

"Sure, you can," Lou said with a taunting smile. "You just have to move on and find someone else."

I grabbed Iris's hand and threaded my fingers through hers. "Here, look, Lou. I've found someone else. Now will you please go back from whence you came?" Iris retracted her hand from my clammy grip and shook it out like a cat who'd just touched wet grass. "Not helping," I muttered from the corner of my mouth.

"Iris is practically your sister," Lou said. "You two would never. Guess you've gotta find someone else to fall in love with."

"Wait." I held up a finger in protest. "You said I need to move on, not fall in love."

"You have to fall in love?" Iris looked between me and the direction of my gaze, despite the fact that she couldn't see Lou.

"That's what moving on means." Lou shrugged. "You've got to fix what you couldn't do with us: admit your feelings instead of running away."

"You can't just stay here!" I shouted, waving around the shop.

Iris flipped the pages of the old spell book. "There's got to be some way to undo this."

"There is," Lou singsonged. She bent down and picked up Ichabod, the sweet cat purring in her arms.

"Holy hell," Iris said, staring at Ichabod.

"Lou, put him down before a customer walks in and sees a levitating black cat," I gritted out. "There's magical and then there's *magical*, and this is the latter. You'll scare away the tourists."

Lou gave Ichabod a kiss on his midnight-black head and placed him on the floor again. He attempted to weave through her legs but went straight through them.

"How do you switch the touching thing on and off?" I asked, and Lou gave me a look. I rolled my eyes. "Let me guess, another afterlife secret you're not allowed to tell me?"

"Yep."

"Ugh," Iris chimed in at the same time. "I never liked her."

Lou blew Iris a kiss that Iris clearly couldn't see. "I knew."

"Just play with the cat."

Iris arched an eyebrow at me. "Lou wants to help you find someone else?"

I nodded.

"Well, that's a first." She twirled a strand of hair

contemplatively. "Are you sure it's not for some other reason? Ghosts aren't infallible."

I cringed. "She seems pretty adamant. But I mean . . . I guess I can go on one date with someone. That might be easier than finding some sort of spell to send her back against her will, right?"

"Hey!" Lou shouted. "Don't you dare."

"It's risky," Iris said at the same time. "If you anger a liminal spirit, it could make her malevolent."

Iris closed the big book. "There's nothing that can help us in here. I'm going to Bones and Tomes to see what I can find." With a groan, she lifted the grimoire back into her arms and headed toward the door. "We're going to need some serious spell work to get rid of this bitch," Iris grumbled.

"Thank you!" I called after her through cupped hands.

She paused, her back holding the door wide open. "It's no worse than that time you saved me from that terrible mix-up with the mugroot." I let out a light laugh at that. "Witches stick together. We'll find a way to fix this, Jordyn."

When she left, Lou looked back at me with a smile. "You already know how to fix this."

"I can't just fall in love on command to get rid of you," I said, combing an exasperated hand through my hair. "There's not exactly a bevy of queer women floating about town. I can't just snap my fingers and have one stumble through the door."

At that very moment, a girl in sage-green overalls covered by a familiar apron walked in the door. She had a shaggy wolf cut, a nose ring, and a bisexual pride flag pinned to her jean jacket.

Lou arched a brow at me, her smile turning wicked.

33

"Don't you fucking dare," I said under my breath before I fled into the back room.

6

HARLOW

W hat was it with jingling doors in this town? Every shop seemed to have a string of golden bells above the door. Was that a superstition thing? Did it ward off bad spirits? Or was it just part of the spooky theme?

The apothecary was eerily quiet.

"Hello?" I tentatively asked the silent room.

The place felt like it was from another time with its towering shelves of bottles and potions, bundles of dried herbs hanging in the window, and the tall ladders on bronze wheels on either side of the room. In the center was a long table with little baskets of herbs and spices arranged around a mortar and pestle. I hoped ground cloves was one of the options.

A soft meow near my ankle caught my attention, and I looked down to find a black cat purring like a motor beneath the table.

"Please tell me you're not the owner," I said to the cat, crouching down and offering my hand to let him smell me.

He rubbed his cheek against my fingertips, and I scratched behind his ear.

A sudden crash sounded from somewhere above me, and I shot up so quickly that I smacked my head on the table ledge. I rubbed the sore spot that would inevitably turn into a goose egg.

I searched for the source of the noise, and my eyes landed on a small glass bottle lying splintered in the middle of the floor, bright-green dust scattered around it.

Fuck. Had I done that? Why was I cursed to be the clumsiest fool alive?

I walked over to the mess and reached out to start picking it up when a hand snapped out of thin air and grabbed my wrist.

"Don't touch that," a honeyed voice commanded.

I pulled away from the warm touch to come face-to-face with the most gorgeous woman I'd ever seen. She had long brown hair that was tucked behind both ears, copper wire-rimmed glasses, a button nose, and rich hazel eyes, a kaleidoscope of greens and ambers within them. Were it not for the tight pinch of her mouth and her narrowed, suspicious eyes, I would've kept gawking, but instead I dropped my gaze and took a step back.

"S-sorry," I said. "I don't know how it happened, but I'll pay for it."

"It wasn't your fault," she replied tightly before she went to fetch a broom and dustpan. "Things have a way of falling off the shelf here lately."

I could've sworn she glared at the cat, who was now weaving a figure eight around nothing at all.

"It wasn't the cat," I quickly added.

"I know." She began sweeping the broken glass and

green powder into a pile, careful not to touch it. "Ichabod knows better."

"Ichabod," I crooned, already falling in love with the sweet black cat. "That is such a cute name."

She hummed in reply.

I tipped my head toward the pile of glass and green dust. "What would've happened if I'd touched that?"

"You would've turned into a toad," the woman replied dryly while she swept the pile into a dustpan. Then she turned away, taking everything with her. I swallowed a lump in my throat and wiped my clammy hands down my jean jacket. "That was a joke," she added over her shoulder.

"Yeah, duh, I know." I feigned a laugh. It was very clear that I did not, in fact, know it was a joke. "I'm just getting used to the whole 'magic is real' thing."

She paused and glanced up at me from where she was tucking away the broom and dustpan. God, those eyes were mesmerizing. I wondered what sort of creature she was, this girl with the hypnotic eyes. Maybe some sort of siren?

"Who are you?" she asked.

"Oh, I'm Harlow, Willow Miller's sister?" My voice cracked and I cleared my throat, trying to lower it back down an octave. "She owns Witch's Brew Café?"

The woman's eyes slid over me in a way that made me uneasy. "I didn't realize Willow had a sister."

"I'm a bit of a wild card. Or black sheep, really." I fixed the hem of my apron nervously. "She was always our parents' favorite. Probably because after high school, I moved out and I've been all over the place. I actually just moved here. She's letting me work in her café, which was a really nice thing to do since she and I had kind of lost touch, which is really my fault. I'm kind of useless at replying to people and I'm . . . blabbing my life story to a total stranger. Sorry."

"It's fine," the woman said, although her expression was one of stone as she glared at the table again.

I instinctively edged away from it. Did she see a spider or something that I didn't?

"No," she said.

"Uh, no what?" I asked.

She blinked and her gaze snapped from the table back to me. "Sorry." She shook her head as if clearing her thoughts. "I'm Jordyn. One of the local witches."

"Jordyn," I echoed. The name suited her. She had a smart, bookish, and—maybe I was overreaching—slightly queer vibe, like an Oxford professor and a Chapstick lesbian had a baby.

God, I really hoped she was gay. That would be amazing. Move to a new town. Find a hot girl. Who was a literal witch. Perfect.

I hadn't really had high hopes that I'd be able to find any dates in a tiny place like Maple Hollow . . . and maybe—probably—I was getting *way* too far ahead of myself.

Did witches even date? Was she queer, or was she just magical? Although a lot of times, it felt like the same thing.

Jordyn said something too low for me to hear, and I moved back to browsing the shelves. My eyes kept snagging on her—her high-waisted charcoal trousers that hugged her slender frame, her chunky cardigan, and tight black tank top that showed off her gorgeous curves.

Was it weird to think that someone had the perfect-sized boobs for their body?

Okay, that was weird.

I needed to stop acting so chaotic.

I tried to focus on the bottles in front of me instead of

the beautiful brunette. Maybe I was focusing a little too closely, though, or maybe she could teleport because the next thing I knew, she was standing right beside me.

"Constipation?" she asked.

My eyes flared as I whirled to her. "Excuse me?"

"Those bottles," she said, pointing with a dainty finger, "are for constipation."

I looked back at the shelf, then immediately turned away as if it had burned my retinas. "No, sorry! I got distracted by the flowers on the label. I'm a bit of a magpie for shiny objects. I see something pretty and I . . ."

My words died on my tongue when my eyes met hers. She was so calm, so still and serene, like a pond without a single ripple. The complete opposite of my jittery nerves. My heart tap-danced just at the sight of her.

I cleared my throat. "Cloves. Willow sent me over to fetch more cloves." I fumbled in my pocket and extended out the now-crumpled twenty-dollar bill my sister had given me.

"I'll grab it for you. Finely ground, I'm assuming?"

I nodded, and Jordyn took the money, her fingers skimming across mine and zapping me with an electric shock. Jordyn and I both jolted backward, and she cracked a half smile as I laughed.

"I swear I haven't been shuffling my socks across the carpet," I said. I was sure my face had turned an unseemly shade of crimson.

Could I be any more awkward? Probably. But I didn't want to try and prove a point to myself.

Jordyn seemed entirely unfazed, which I was beginning to suspect was a normal trait for her. "Must be some static in the air," she mused as she wandered toward the till and made some change. She shot a sharp look to her side again, scowling at the wall, and I inched backward, wondering if the place was haunted or something.

I toyed with the little pendants hanging from a branch by the register. One had a carving of a mouse in the center of a stained-glass triangle. "What is this for?"

"To ward off pests," Jordyn said, not even looking at the trinkets.

"How does it work?"

Jordyn looked at me like the answer was obvious, like everyone knew how to use magical pendants. "You spin it around three times and then hang it in the window facing out to keep them out."

I gave her a tight grin. "Right." She was so gorgeous that I was forgetting how to use words.

"Do you want one?" she asked in a flat tone, which told me that she wanted me to go away.

"Oh, uh. . ." I fiddled with them. I supposed it wouldn't hurt to ward off mice from the café. "Sure." I plucked the one hanging from a purple satin ribbon and placed it on the countertop.

Jordyn grabbed a brown paper bundle from a shelf behind her and passed it to me. This time, our fingertips didn't have a chance to touch since she practically dropped the bag into my waiting palms.

I hugged it to my chest. "Thanks."

"It was nice to meet you, Harlow." She flashed me a tight smile. "I hope you come again sometime."

I was bad at reading these situations. Why was she talking to me like she had a knife to her back?

"It was nice meeting you too," I said warily, though her full pink lips momentarily distracted me from her robotic movements. I should not be thinking about her lips when she was clearly annoyed by me. "Okay, bye!" I turned to flee.

Unfortunately, the cat, who I was certain had been across the room just a second ago, was directly under my feet, and I tripped to avoid stepping on him. As I threw my arms out, a hand caught me by the elbow, stalling my fall.

"Sorry. Sorry!" I exclaimed, whirling in Jordyn's arms.

Surprise widened her eyes, but something else was there too. But before I could decrypt whatever emotions were whirling through her, Jordyn hastily released me and folded her arms tight around her torso.

"It was my fault," she said, sounding almost dejected. "Or rather, Ichabod's."

"Sorry, Ichabod," I offered. I bent down to give the cat a quick scratch, and he purred and arched into my hand.

At least he wasn't giving me the ice queen treatment.

Careful not to trip over Ichabod a second time, I turned and left, stealing one last look through the window to see the gorgeous girl glaring at the wall again.

7

JORDYN

I paced the length of the shop, fuming. "First, you break an expensive bottle of elixir. Then you get her to nearly trample my cat!" I glared at Lou, wishing she were corporeal so I could strangle her. Harlow probably thought I was some weird townie who didn't know how to hold a conversation. I didn't want to think too hard about how true that was.

"He was fine," Lou said, waving her hand at Ichabod, who'd gone back to lounging in the sun. Lou seemed completely unfazed by the absolute lunacy she'd caused. "He knew how to play his part. *You*, on the other hand, are completely hopeless."

"And what part was that? The creepy shop owner who hits on her customers the first time they visit the store?" I hissed, remembering the way I'd grabbed Harlow's elbow to keep her from falling over . . . and the way my touch had *lingered*. "And how was I even supposed to have anything close to a conversation with her while you were there yapping for only me to hear?"

"She was into you," Lou countered in a teasing tone. "She was totally checking you out when you had your back turned."

I pinched the bridge of my nose. "Lou, it's weird enough that you're here. I don't need you telling me when other girls are checking me out."

"Although I think you put her off with all your glowering at me. You need to get a handle on the looking-at-nothing thing."

"And whose fault is that?" I rolled my eyes and muttered a few choice words.

Lou floated to the top of our tall display cabinet to fiddle with the bottles on the top shelf, adjusting the labels so they were in a perfect line. "I see now that I have my work cut out for me. Who put the wolfsbane next to the wormwood shavings?"

"They're literally in alphabetical order." I cocked my hip and planted a hand on it. "And don't worry, you won't have to deal with our inventory once Iris gets back here with the right coven spell books to send you back."

"Speak of the devil," Lou said, eyeing the redhead through the window. She floated toward the door on silent footsteps and opened it wide for Iris, who rushed through with her hands full of heavy books stacked up to her angular chin.

"Thanks, Lou," Iris said over her shoulder.

Apparently, she had gotten over the whole ghost-haunting-her-best-friend-thing faster than I'd thought she would.

Iris set the books down on the long table and turned around. "Alright, I brought over all the general spell books on spirits, possessions, and hauntings that I could find. But first things first."

I fixed my gaze on her stony expression and waited for her to go on.

"Who was that hottie in the jean jacket and café apron?" Iris asked. "I didn't know there was someone new in town."

"That was Harlow, Willow's sister," I said. "And I am *not* asking her out," I added emphatically to Lou.

Iris swept a lock of hair behind her ear. "You're sure?"

"I am *very* sure that I made the impression that I am undateable." I pursed my lips and exhaled a sigh, hoping neither of them would press the matter.

Iris thought for a moment. "So you don't mind if I ask her out, then?"

That question shouldn't have bothered me in the slightest, and the answer I should have given clashed with the urge to shout that I'd seen her first. Harlow was this crazy mix of quirky and fun and beautiful. Unlike the people in this town who leaned toward the macabre, she was a walking rainbow unicorn. White-blonde hair, bright blue eyes, gorgeous plumps lips, and a perfectly athletic build with the forearms of a rock climber and . . .

Fuck. It had been *way* too long since I'd been pressed up against another body.

"Cat got your tongue?" Lou taunted.

"No," I spat, "it doesn't."

"What doesn't?" Iris's brow quirked.

I groaned and scrubbed my hand down my face. "I'm sick of this game of telephone! Stop talking!"

"Me?" Iris asked.

"Not you. Lou," I growled and turned back to the books on the table. "New rule: ghosts stay silent!"

"Yeah, that's not happening." Lou chuckled, but to her credit, she did quiet down.

For the next few hours, we pored over every page in each of the spell books while Lou watched from the air. And then while dangling from one of the overhead lights. *And then* from the top of the elixir cupboard. Before she ended up floating in the air above my head, humming the tune to a Hozier song.

Iris and I tried a dozen hexes, counter-curses, and cleansing rituals, but all we did was use up ingredients from the back room. At least Lou wasn't turning into a malevolent spirit. *But* she also wasn't returning to the after-life. With each failed incantation, my heart sank a little more.

Maybe she really was here until I moved on to a new love. *Goddess, please don't let that be it.* It was torture of mythological proportions to have Lou follow me around as I tried to woo someone else.

Iris swept up some bright red and yellow powders from the floor after yet another failed spell. "We're going to need more salt if we're going to try again."

"Don't bother." I huffed, shutting the book I was flipping through with a dull thud. We'd already used a bucketful, and the impending cleanup was only adding to my annoyance. "We're reaching with these spells. We need something more powerful."

"We can do darker, but I don't think that's the sort of magic you want to tempt onto this plane," Iris assured me.

"I know, you're right," I grumbled. "Thanks for helping me try."

She gave me a bright smile. "You know I love this stuff. Beats refilling bottles and replying to emails."

"True." I chuckled.

"You already know how to get rid of me, Jords," Lou said in a teasing singsong.

I rolled my eyes.

Iris studied my face and frowned. "She's really giving you hell, isn't she?"

"You have no idea." I rubbed the tomes' dust from my aching eyes.

"Just go ask her out," Lou pushed. "One date."

I balled up my fists and set my knuckles on the table.

Iris huffed. "What did she say?"

"She wants me to ask Harlow out," I repeated loud enough to make a point. "A woman I don't even know, might I add."

"I mean . . . ," Iris hedged with raised shoulders.

I pinned my supposed best friend with an aggrieved stare. "Not you too."

Iris spread another spell book across the table. "If it's only going to take one date, then that's easier than me spending days hunting down a spell."

"You just said that you love hunting down spells," I countered.

"I do," she conceded. "But you might as well try option B while I'm painstakingly sifting through hundreds of years of texts for you, okay?"

"Ugh. The guilt!"

She was right, of course. Which only made Lou giggle at my defeat.

"The worst she can do is say no," Iris said. "Why are you so reluctant to ask this girl out?"

"Yeah," Lou added. "Why?"

I threw my hands up in the air. "Okay, fine! You win!" I grabbed my coat off the chair behind the counter. "I'll go ask her out." I pointed to Iris. "But you keep working on the spells in case of the very real possibility that I come back with crushing rejection stamped on my face."

Iris nodded.

"And you." I rounded on Lou. "Stay here with her."

Lou cackled as she followed me to the door. "No way! I have to see this for myself. How else will my soul know you're putting in effort?"

8

HARLOW

When I got back to the café, I gave Willow the bag of ground cloves with a confident nod. I hadn't managed to mess up the first thing she'd trusted me with, and the small, grateful smile she gave me was my reward.

After the crowd started to thin, I stepped out from behind the counter to bus tables. I couldn't help but look out the window. I took the pendant out of my pocket. When no one was watching, I spun it around three times and hung it behind the curtain in the window, the cute little mouse face staring at me. This was fun—this quaint, little magic. Maybe this town was growing on me.

I had just turned back to clear another table when someone shrieked, "Mice!"

My stomach dropped as more shrieks erupted and patrons leaped up onto the tables or started fleeing the building altogether. Willow grabbed the broom and rushed around the countertop, but then her eyes filled with horror.

A river of mice was streaming in through the front and back doors and dispersing into every corner of the café.

"Holy shit!" I hissed. "Did I do it wrong?"

Willow whipped her head toward me. "What did you do?" Willow shouted.

"It was meant to ward off pests!"

But the place had been overrun with vermin in a matter of seconds. Now, the air was full of their squeaking and scuttling.

"What? Where?"

I pointed to the curtain, and Willow rushed over and retrieved the pendant from behind it. She plucked it up and sent the small trinket twirling before hanging it back up. The mice magically reversed course as quickly as they'd come.

"You face the mouse *out!*" Willow growled at me once they'd all gone. "So they stay out!"

"You say that like it's obvious," I snapped back. "How was I supposed to know that?" Other than the fact that the pretty girl at the apothecary had told me, but I wasn't about to tell my sister that.

"You could've at least told me before you hung it up in my window and scared off all of my customers." She huffed, wiping her hands with a damp towel.

"I'm sorry!" I watched as the last little tail disappeared under the front door, my chest heaving with the panic of the moment.

Willow pinched the bridge of her nose. "I don't want you to be sorry," she hissed. "I want you to *ask* before you make decisions that affect *my* livelihood, for fuck's sake, Harlow!"

I winced. "I'll clean it up," I promised and turned to go fetch the mop. "I'll make it right."

Willow deflated at that, but she didn't say another word as she took to the street to tell people they could return to the café after we'd cleaned up. I also heard her say the incident was my fault.

After sweeping, mopping, and polishing, the café was back to pre-mouse levels of pristine. And by the time the late-afternoon lull before closing hit, I took a moment to lie across the rust-colored vinyl of a booth, a dishtowel draped across my eyes. I'd never cleaned so much in my life.

How did Willow do this every single day? I mean, the café was closed on Mondays, but she still used that day to balance her books and do a stock inventory. I had a newfound respect for my sister. She was a machine. She was also a natural with every customer—local or tourist—who came in to the café. She greeted everyone with a smile and took care of them like a friend. The clockwork transactions, order fulfillment, and pleasantries made my sister glow with a happiness that was infectious.

Throughout the day, different patrons would come in and I'd made a game of guessing what kind of creature they were. It was pretty easy to tell the tourists apart from the magical town residents once you had an eye for it. Dressing up in costume and taking photos of everything was a dead giveaway.

In the end, it came down to "no selfies equals local." Easy as that.

The door jangled open, and I wanted to shout, "Be right with you!" but I was too tired to even summon the will to speak. I wanted to rot in bed for a week after today. If a demon had just walked in to steal my soul, then so be it. At least then I could rest.

But then I heard a familiar voice say, "Uh, Harlow?"

With a start, I flung the towel across the booth and bolted upright like I'd been zapped with defibrillators.

"Jordyn! Uh, hey." I dusted my hair out of my eyes and smoothed down my wrinkled apron. I knew my attempts at nonchalance were futile after my dramatic reawakening. "What's up?"

Jordyn hugged her arms to her chest, her expression stoic if not outright angry. In the space between one breath and the next, I ran through the Rolodex of reasons she could have for coming here. Did she want me to pay for that broken bottle after all? Did I injure Ichabod?

"I was, um, wondering"—she shifted back and forth on her feet, her stony demeanor ruffling around the edges—"since you're new in town . . . if you wanted someone to show you around? Maybe we could go to Midnight Market and grab some ice cream and walk around the town together? I mean, if you're free. I'm sure Willow could show you around, too, if you, uh, didn't want to."

"Oh." I tried—and failed—to hide my surprise. "Yes. I mean, no."

Her face fell. "No?"

"No, Willow can't show me around. She's too busy," I clumsily clarified. "I'd really like to have you show me around. Thanks for offering!"

Jordyn's shoulders slumped, but her sour expression lifted. "How about tomorrow after you close up?"

I watched the way she bounced on her toes. Maybe she pitied me? Had someone asked her to do this? Was this a guilt thing? Or was she just nervous? I had no idea. But getting ice cream with a gorgeous girl was definitely not a hardship. And if we were together, that hopefully meant no monster would eat me while I explored the town so . . . win-win, right?

"That sounds great." I beamed, overcompensating for my nerves with aggressive optimism.

I wasn't convinced that Jordyn was entirely enthused by my answer, but then the tone of her voice shifted to relief when she said, "Great. I'll come by tomorrow around this time?"

"Perfect," I replied with a smile. "I promise to try to be slightly more put together than I am now."

Her tight grin morphed into what felt like a real smile. "It's a date."

She left before that comment could register in my brain. I waited until she walked past the streetlight and around the corner before I let out a squeal of glee and frolicked about the café with enough energy to push through the final items on my to-do list before officially closing the shop for the night.

"Someone has a second wind," Willow said as she carted in a clean tray of coffee cups from the kitchen.

Her previous cold shoulder had melted once I'd cleaned up the mess I'd made. She wasn't ready to laugh about it *yet*, but I knew it was coming.

"I just got asked on a date," I replied, twirling whimsically.

Willow's head reared back like I'd just told her I was pregnant with Jack Skellington's baby. "By whom?"

"The girl who works at the apothecary," I sang.

Willow smiled. "Iris? She's adorable. That's so cute!"

"No, the brunette," I corrected. "Her name's Jordyn?"

Willow's expression warred between surprise and confusion. "I wasn't expecting that."

My cheer dampened. "Why not?"

Willow shrugged. "It's not a bad thing. Jordyn's great, but she's a bit of a recluse. Definitely introverted. As far as I know, she hasn't dated anyone since she and her girlfriend broke up last year. If I'm remembering right, Lou passed away shortly after in a car accident."

I didn't know what to do with that information, but it sparked a hundred questions like: *Was that why Jordyn was so standoffish? Or was she just rusty after such a long dating hiatus? Did it take a year to mend her broken heart?*

It didn't matter. The fact that Jordyn wanted to spend time with me was enough.

"Well, she offered to show me around town, and I figured I'd be safer with her. Right?"

Weighing her head from side to side, Willow pursed her lips. "I mean, that's probably true."

"And she's a witch?"

My sister shot me a look. "You didn't think to find that out *before* you agreed to go on a date with her?"

"She told me she was a witch already. I'm just confirming," I said defensively. Although if she hadn't told me, I still would've said yes. "And she's cute!"

Willow shook her head at my hopeless antics. Resting her hands on her hips, Willow said, "Yes, she's a witch. And a powerful one at that. Be careful."

"A powerful witch," I said with a little shimmy. "That's hot." Then I started thinking of the implications of that. "Maybe she'll cast a love spell on me. She can't turn me into a newt or something, can she?"

"You know what? I'm going to let you figure that out for yourself. Serves you right for agreeing to go on a date with someone from this town without knowing who or what they are first." Willow waved her dishtowel at me as she dried out the still-steaming glasses.

I gawked at her. "You'd let your baby sister go out with an evil witch just to prove a point?"

"You're so dramatic." She rolled her eyes. "Jordyn's a good person. She won't put a hex on you or anything like that."

"Whew."

"It'll be good to get to know the town with a local too," Willow offered. "Everyone seeing you with her will mean you're under the coven's protection. Off-limits."

"Off-limits?" I asked. "Off-limits to—" I held up two fingers and hooked them against my neck like a vampire sucking blood. Willow nodded, and my mouth fell open. "So . . . how many tourists come here and never return home?"

Willow wrinkled her nose. "I think it's best not to ask that."

"What!"

"Oh, and if you have any customers give you grief, you tell me and I'll tell Wyatt. The pack loves picking off assholes who don't tip."

I gaped at her. "Who are you and what have you done with my pacifist sister?"

Willow winked and disappeared into the back room to finish up prep for tomorrow, leaving me to wonder what in her time here had made her so strong.

9
JORDYN

The next day, after fulfilling yesterday's orders and stocking the shelves, Iris and I marched into the Maple Hollow police station with Lou following behind.

"This is pointless. You should be getting ready for your date instead of trying to solve my death," Lou balked for the hundredth time. "Which, by the way, I still have not asked you to do."

"Shh!" I hissed as we walked up to the counter.

She wasn't wrong about that, but I couldn't take the chance that Lou would linger if there was any question that her death really wasn't an accident.

The Maple Hollow police station was very small and filled with police officers who were used to evading unseemly questions about disappearing tourists. The wolf pack took turns manning the desk, just like my coven took turns running the apothecary. Werewolves—apparently— made excellent police officers.

Dougall McCleighton manned the desk today. He sat at

attention for a second until he realized I wasn't an out-of-towner and then drooped back down to do his crossword puzzle.

"Is the coven having problems with the raccoon population again?" Dougall asked. "I can sic the pack on them if you'd like?"

"No." I sighed. "We're not here on coven business."

That piqued his interest. "Oh yeah? What do you need, ladies?"

I cringed at his eagerness to be the wolf in shining armor. Witches didn't need wolves in shining armor. But in this matter, we did need the police.

"Were you around during that car crash that killed Lou Wong?" I did my best to sound sweet and not demanding.

Dougall pursed his lips and nodded solemnly. "Yeah, I was at the crash site. Terrible business."

"I really don't want to dredge this up, Jords," Lou grumbled, a twinge of pain in her voice.

"Then go wait outside," I whispered.

"What?" Dougall perked his ears.

I really needed to stop talking to Lou, especially around werewolves and their super hearing abilities.

"Just praying to the Moon Goddess!" Iris said, covering for me as she whispered some nonsensical words under her breath.

Dougall shook his head. "Witches."

"Was there anything suspicious about the crash?" I asked.

"Nah," Dougall said. "Looked like she passed out while behind the wheel. The car veered off into a ditch. All the upholstery reeked of alcohol. Clearly drunk driving."

"I was sober," Lou said with disbelief. "I hadn't had a drink in years."

"What did her toxicology report say?" I asked. "How far over the limit was she?" I knew he wouldn't know off the top of his head. What I wanted was for him to produce the reports for me.

Dougall eyed me suspiciously. "Why are you so concerned about this? It was a year ago?"

Iris quickly wrapped her arms around me as I fumbled for an answer. "Come on, Dougall, haven't you ever lost someone close to you? Jordyn needs closure. Can't you help us out? Please?" She was too good at those puppy eyes.

"Ah, right," Dougall said. "I'd forgotten you two were a thing."

"You're not the only one," Lou mumbled.

"Well, you'll have to ask Rudy about those reports." He hooked a thumb behind him in the direction of the coroner's office.

"Okay, we'll go ask Rudy." Iris started steering me away. "Thanks, Dougall."

"I hope you get what you need for peace, Jordyn," Dougall called after us. I turned and looked at him. "Such a sad thing, seeing that car in the ditch in the middle of the day like that. Seems like she'd been in a bad way."

"No, I wasn't," Lou snarled. She clenched her hands into fists and stomped, and her boot collided with the wood floor, making us all jump.

Iris doubled over, pretending to cough and stomp her foot. "Ah, seasonal allergies," she said, practically dragging me out the door. "Thanks again!"

She pulled me across the street and down a side alley, away from the prying eyes of the tourists teeming through the main square. "We are trying to prevent a malevolent spirit! Dragging Lou"—she waved at the air beside her—

"around to investigate her death is only going to exacerbate the situation."

I pointed at Lou. "She's on your other side." Iris opened her mouth, but I just pushed on. "I'm going on my date with Harlow tonight. We won't have to worry about what she'll do for much longer. It just seems weird, don't you think?"

"I guess, but you and Lou were on the outs at the time. It's not like she would have told you that she was planning to go on a bender and then drive into town."

"Lou wouldn't do that. Ever." My voice cracked, and I looked at Lou. "Do you want me to keep digging or not?"

Lou drew her shoulders up, holding them there for a long moment before letting them drop low, defeated. It was the same shrug she'd used when she hadn't wanted to choose what movie we watched or what pizza we ordered. Back then, her stubborn indecisiveness had been cute, now I wasn't too sure how to feel. She'd always let me lead, and I knew this was my last chance to do something meaningful for her.

"It's settled, then. I'm going to talk to Rudy." I nodded to Lou, who gave me a small smile.

"I bet Dougall didn't want to do a conclusive investigation," Lou said.

I snorted. "That sounds like him. He's all too familiar with doing that for missing tourists."

Iris snapped her fingers in front of my face. "Hello! Care to clue in the living over here?"

"Sorry, I know this seems crazy to you, but I have to find out what really happened. Even if Lou passes back over after my date tonight."

Iris sighed. "Fine. Of course, I'll help. Not that you asked, but I'm invested now."

"Thanks," Lou and I said at once.

Iris and I fell into step with each other as we headed toward the coroner's office. If we were lucky, Rudy would still be around and able to look into Lou's files.

At the time, I'd only heard that Lou had been in a bad accident and that they'd assumed she'd been headed into town. No one had mentioned the smell of alcohol or that they'd suspected that she'd fallen asleep at the wheel. The time of death hadn't been published in the obituary, but it had been odd that it had happened in the middle of the day but there had been no other vehicles involved. Had there been witnesses? Or perhaps someone else in the car with Lou?

Dougall not knowing much about the accident seemed off as well. He wasn't the most intuitive guy around, but I would have thought the police department would have tried to dig a little more. Perhaps if Lou had been a tourist, it would have made sense that her accident had been brushed under the rug, but she was *from* Maple Hollow. Her parents had been part of the demonic council. Something wasn't sitting right at all.

Maybe Rudy would have some answers for me. But before we could round the corner and head to his office, the café door blasted open and a woman screamed, "Help! Someone, call a doctor!"

Iris and I exchanged glances as my heartbeat kicked up to a thunderous tempo. My first thought was that I hoped it wasn't Harlow, but I pushed that aside as Iris and I lurched into a full-out run.

10

HARLOW

I hovered over the collapsed elderly woman as she lay flat on her back on the café floor. Her snakelike canines gleamed as her mouth opened and closed like a fish. Willow hurriedly shoved the other patrons out the door to make room for the medical emergency.

When everyone was gone, I shouted to my sister, "What is she?"

"Vampire!" Willow shouted back as she let Wyatt run in.

"I heard the screaming. What's wrong?" he asked, looking around frantically for the cause of the distress.

"It's Agnes." Willow pointed at the woman. "I think she's going into anaphylactic shock or something."

"*Can* vampires go into anaphylactic shock?" I asked.

"Apparently!" Willow wailed, pacing around as Agnes's eyes started to roll back.

"Agnes." I reached down to grip the woman's shoulder. "Help's coming. Stay awake. She reeks of alcohol. Maybe she's drunk?" I darted looks between Willow and Wyatt. "She should stay awake, right? I don't know vampire CPR!"

"She probably just fed off a drunk person," my sister said. "That's not what this is!"

"Well, I'm sorry I missed the vampire episode of *Grey's Anatomy*!" I shouted. "I don't know what to do!"

"I don't know what to do either!" Willow cried, her hands racking through her hair.

"Hey, hey. She's going to be okay," Wyatt said, circling his arms around Willow and pulling her into his broad chest. "I saw some witches running across the square. They're almost here."

"Witches?" I looked up right as the café door opened and Jordyn and Iris stepped in like dark academia superheroes.

"Move!" the redhead shouted.

I scooted backward as the two witches knelt on either side of Agnes. Jordyn took a small vial of something from her messenger bag and uncorked it, and then she poured a strong-smelling liquid through the vampire's cracked lips. But it didn't seem to do any good.

I held my breath, and Jordyn and her friend joined hands and closed their eyes. They murmured something in Latin over and over, their voices growing louder, as if they were battling something away with their chanting. The still air of the café came alive, warping and bending around them, swirling up toward the wooden beams above.

Agnes's eyes flared open, and she sucked down a giant gulp of air. Before my very eyes, the swollen red spots on Agnes's face shrank and her mottled complexion returned to its smooth, pale porcelain.

I had the overwhelming urge to ask if vampires really needed to breathe, but I kept my mouth closed.

"Steady," Jordyn said as she hooked an arm under Agnes's armpit and helped her into a seated position.

It was probably not an appropriate time to think Jordyn

looked incredibly sexy, but I couldn't help but gawk at how calm and confident she was. The adrenaline coursing through me was probably twisting my emotions, but seeing her save someone's life with her magic was incredible.

The redheaded witch rested a hand on Agnes's arm. "What happened?"

"I have no idea," Agnes said once her breathing had steadied. She smoothed down her black satin dress and rose to stand as if levitating on thin air. She was back to the preternatural creature she had been only moments before I'd served her. "I just ordered my normal cappuccino. The new girl served it to me."

Everyone's eyes landed on me. I wished harder than ever before that the ground would open under my feet and swallow me whole. Could Jordyn make me disappear? Or teleport me out of there? That would've been a miracle.

"What did you give her?" Willow's voice was filled with accusation.

"Nothing," I rasped. "I just made the cappuccino like you showed me and sprinkled it with cocoa powder and . . ." My stomach plummeted as I realized what I'd done.

"And?" Willow snapped, and Wyatt's arms tightened around her.

"And I added a festive dash of cinnamon and nutmeg on top?"

Agnes clasped her hands together, her frown growing sharp and vicious like I was her next meal. "I'm allergic to nutmeg."

"I-I-I'm so sorry." I scrambled to find the words. "I didn't even know vampires could have allergies!"

"You could've asked," Agnes said coldly. She turned her violent red gaze to Willow. "I will tell the others to think twice before coming back here again. I knew we shouldn't have allowed humans in this town."

"Oh, Agnes, I'm so sorry," Willow pleaded. "I promise it won't happen again. It was a mistake. I'll do all of the orders from now on—"

Agnes held up her hand, cutting off Willow's words. She eyed the witches. "Thank you, ladies." She glared at me one more time then left.

Willow shoved out of Wyatt's grip, her face a new shade of crimson as she seethed at me. "I'd like to speak with my sister alone, please," she snarled.

"Is now an inappropriate time to tell you you're hot when you're angry?" Wyatt whispered.

My sister shot him a look, and he folded in an instant. He looked at the witches, beckoned them with a hand, and they all turned to leave.

"Go easy on her," Wyatt added as he headed out the door. "She didn't know."

I gave him a silent look of thanks even as I shrank an inch out of shame with every belabored breath I took. I looked up just as Jordyn averted her gaze from mine. I had a terrible feeling our date was off. Nothing like accidentally killing a local to ruin the mood. The witches left without any further comment and Willow just stood there, chest heaving until the door closed behind her.

"Wills, I'm sorry—"

"You almost killed one of the oldest vampires in town!" Willow screamed so loud that people walking past the windows paused and stared.

"How was I supposed to know I could kill a vampire with nutmeg of all things? It's ridiculous!" I shouted back. "Garlic, crucifixes, stakes, sure. You're acting like I was trying to serve her a steaming mug of holy water! If anything, *you* should've prepared me for this."

"So it's my fault?" Willow snarled, looking like she wanted to punch a hole in the wall.

"No, I just mean that—"

"Now all of the vampires will be boycotting my café. You have no idea how much you've just hurt my business! What if they get the demons to stop coming too?"

"Are demons allergic to anything?"

"This isn't funny, Harlow!" she shouted, and I swore she was two seconds from having steam curl out of her ears. "I worked so hard to build this place, to gain the locals' trust, and you come in here and in *two days* you fuck it up like you always do!"

I winced at that, her words stinging more than a slap in the face. My biggest fear was coming true right before my very eyes. I choked back the sting in my throat and the welling tears. The heat of embarrassment at being scolded mixed with the dread in my belly that she was going to send me away. I wiped away the streams wetting my cheeks.

Willow put a hand to her chest and took a steeling breath. "I'm sorry. That's harsher than I intended, but for fuck's sake, Harlow."

"No, you're right." The words came out hollow. "I fucked everything up."

"You're on cleanup and kitchen duty for the foreseeable future. I will handle the customer side of things from now on."

"You're not kicking me out?" I asked, surprised.

Her eyes saddened. "No. I'm not kicking you out." She offered me a half-hearted smile. "Not yet, at least."

"I really am sorry." I rubbed the chill off my arms. "You know the one good thing about me being around?"

Willow perked a brow and waited for my selling point.

"You're more angry than usual."

She narrowed her eyes at me. "And that's a good thing because?"

I winked at her. "Wyatt thinks you're hot when you're angry."

Her blush flamed across her face as she threw the dish towel at me and strained not to laugh. "Shut up!"

She muttered to herself all the way back to the kitchen.

I chuckled and made to take a step to follow her when the doorbells chimed behind me. Jordyn peeked her head inside, and I had to stop my jaw from hitting the floor.

"Hey."

I cleared my throat and straightened my spine. "Hi."

Smooth, Harlow.

"Are we still on for tonight?" Her face gave away no emotion that I could pin down.

My surprise turned to delight as I nodded. "Yes! I think Willow needs some time to cool off without me around."

I'd been sure she was going to ghost me after what had happened with Agnes. Maybe she pitied me after Willow had laid into me, but I couldn't find a reason to care or question it.

"Cool. See you in a bit then." She ducked out and disappeared down the sidewalk without another word.

My cheeks strained against a foolishly wide smile as I ran to get ready. I was about to go on a date with a witch!

11

JORDYN

I thrust my hands into my pockets, my shoulders bunched around my ears as Lou followed me down the street. I was on my way to pick up Harlow for our date. Long shadows grew over the town square as the late-afternoon sun dipped below the haunted wood.

"Why are you following me?" I muttered to my feet.

I'd finally learned not to look at Lou when speaking to her. Iris had been coaching me all day to act like I didn't have my ex incessantly in my ear.

"You know why I'm here," Lou countered, traipsing along like she was gleefully marching me to my execution.

"I'm moving on, okay?" I gestured in the direction of Witch's Brew Café.

"I'm not going until I'm sure you're not bailing on a good thing. If I wait at the apothecary, you might jump into the bushes at the last second and never even go on this date."

I groaned. "This is none of your business."

"You made it my business when you *summoned* me!"

It dawned on me all at once that we were going to have this same argument for the rest of my fucking life. I could picture it now: me, an old crone, stooped and withered, working in my apothecary with my snarky ex-girlfriend, still in her late twenties and in *my* fucking T-shirt, smugly watching while she waited for me to kick the bucket.

Goddess, I hoped I'd at least be able to get away from her in the afterlife. Maybe she'd haunt me there too . . .

"I'm doing the best I can," I grumbled. "But you clinging to me is not helping. I'm going on this date. Ease up."

"I'll ease up when I see you catching feelings."

"You're going to be waiting a long time." I paused at the door to the Witch's Brew. "The odds of me catching feelings are slim to none. Especially in a single date."

The café door opened and out swept Harlow looking like an androgynous movie star. Her short hair was styled loosely, framing her heart-shaped face. She wore a charcoal-gray shirt unbuttoned dangerously low to allow me little peeks at her lacy black bra. Cuffed black jeans, black combat boots, and a faux-leather bomber jacket completed the look.

Well, fuck.

"You were saying?" Lou asked.

I swatted a hand through her gauzy form and played it off like I was lifting a hand to sweep my hair out of my eyes.

"You look nice," I croaked, my throat suddenly bone-dry.

Harlow's cheeks flushed. "You too."

We held each other's gazes for another second. Her eyes were like a clear winter sky, piercing and beautiful. I wanted to free-fall into them.

Lou snickered as if reading my thoughts, and I straightened. Cleared my throat.

Nope. I wanted none of those things. At least not with my ex-girlfriend's ghost skulking around.

"Ready to explore Maple Hollow?" I asked.

I waited for Harlow to walk down the steps to my side, and then we started walking in stilted silence, taking in the town. Lou, to her credit, stayed a few paces behind, though she was incessantly humming "Call Me Maybe" to herself. Of course. Nothing like having the ghost of your ex humming a merry tune while you're trying to date another girl.

"So," Harlow said tentatively, breaking the silence, "how long have you lived here?"

"My whole life," I said. "I've never lived anywhere else. No real desire to either." Goddess help me, my conversational skills were about as interesting as beige wallpaper.

"No desire to travel?"

"Travel, yes, but I'll always keep a base here, I think. I'd miss my coven too much." I paused. "I told you I was a witch, right?"

"Yes," she said with a laugh.

"Good," I said tightly. "Normally, I'm better at keeping a lid on town secrets, but I guess I'm just, uh, nervous tonight."

Harlow seemed pleased with that answer, taking a step closer to my side. "This whole town makes me nervous," Harlow added, taking in the square. "At first, I was nervous about everyone here hurting me. Now I'm worried I'm going to accidentally hurt them."

"Who would've known a vampire could have a nutmeg allergy?"

"Right?" she exclaimed, and I chuckled. "I mean, of all the things I could've messed up."

"Was Willow really mad?" I asked. "She looked really mad."

"I've been relegated to cleanup and kitchen duty for the foreseeable future."

"Ouch."

"It's my fault. I get it. This place is important to Willow, and I don't want to ruin it for her. I understand now why she loves this place so much. It's certainly magical."

My heart twinged for her. She seemed so dejected that she'd disappointed her sister. "It's not that different than other towns."

"I wouldn't go that far." She let out a laugh, pointing to the gilded store signs dotted around the square. "The Cauldron Candle Shop. Bones and Tomes Bookstore. The Poisoned Apple Apothecary?" She let out a snort, and I pressed my lips together to keep from smiling at her. "Those aren't exactly *normal* shops."

"We really stick to the theme." I gestured to the hair salon. "They're pretty normal."

She eyed the storefront of Luna's Hairdresser, a howling wolf in silver appliqué on the front window. "Let me guess," Harlow said. "They have a discount for werewolves?"

I let out a surprised laugh. "Look at you fitting in like a local already."

"She's adorable!" Lou called from behind me. "I think you should hang on to this one, Jords."

I glared at her over my shoulder, and Harlow paused.

"You okay?" she asked hesitantly. "You seem like you've had something on your mind. Earlier today, too."

"No." I tried to paste on a pleasant smile. "I thought I had a gnat in my ear is all."

"That's a new nickname," Lou said with a low whistle. "Can't say I'm partial to it."

"Here we are!" I said a little too loudly, gesturing to Midnight Market. The storefront was built like a Victorian manor despite it being wedged between two nondescript shops. It was painted in all black and sparkled iridescently like a raven's wings.

I opened the door and Harlow stumbled backward at the sight inside.

"Whoa," I said softly, catching her by the elbow. "You okay?"

"What in the Frankenstein?" she whispered, staring wide-eyed at Billy.

The shop was filled with black shelves holding glass jars of every type of chocolate and confectionary. To the left was the standard grocery store fare and to the right was an ice cream counter with Halloween-themed frozen treats. And manning that counter? Billy Bacchus, mayor of Maple Hollow and owner of the Midnight Market.

Billy had green skin, dark, sunken-in eyes ringed in black, white hair with shocks of black, and various stitches holding his peeling skin together.

A tourist family wearing matching navy-blue puffer vests was at the counter.

"Your costume is incredible," the mother said, inspecting his face as she licked her mint chocolate chip ice cream. "How long does it take to put it all on?"

"Less time than you'd think," Billy said in a deep baritone, his smile wide and genuine.

Harlow was standing half behind me, tucked into my side, and I couldn't help but drape a reassuring arm around her back.

"He's harmless," I whispered.

"Is he like a . . ." She shook her head, clearly coming up short. Her face was turning a similar shade of green to Billy's, and I wondered if she was going to be sick.

"Monster," I offered.

I wasn't about to deep dive into what species of monster. That was probably second-date material.

I peeked at Lou, who was perusing the shelves of treats. Hopefully, she'd be gone by date two.

Did I even want a second date?

"Billy has a knack for charming visitors," I continued. "For the locals, however, he is a constant stick up all of our asses with his ordinances and constant town hall meetings." I leaned in closer to whisper in Harlow's ear. I couldn't help but take in her smell, warm and spicy like cinnamon and mulled cider. Perfect for this place. She smelled like home. "Still, he's kind of like a grandfather figure to most of us."

"So monsters are real and they serve ice cream in little New England towns? Awesome."

"Well, this one does." I nodded toward Billy. I leaned in again, my lips accidentally skimming her ear. "You're taking all of this surprisingly well, you know."

When I pulled back, I saw the ripple of gooseflesh down the back of her neck, and it made me want to whisper in her ear some more. Instead, I cleared my throat and took a definitive step away.

"Coward," Lou snickered.

I held up my middle finger behind my back.

When the family finished ordering, the mother demanded the two kids take a photo with Billy, who seemed all too happy to oblige.

"Have a lovely family vacation," he called with a wave. "And make sure to tell your friends and family to stop by next fall too!"

I rolled my eyes. "Ever the town spokesman, Billy." I wandered over to the counter and took in the offerings. When I looked back, Harlow was still lingering by the door, looking like she might bolt. I took three giant steps back and threaded my fingers with hers.

"What are you—"

I yanked Harlow up to the counter like dragging a reluctant dog out of the park. Her shoes skidded across the tiles until Billy's eyes landed on her. Then she straightened and put on a strained smile.

"Hi!" she squeaked, her voice an octave higher than it had been a second before.

"Billy, meet Harlow, Willow's sister," I said. "Harlow, meet Billy Bacchus, the mayor of Maple Hollow."

Billy extended his hand, and Harlow stared at it, mouth agape, before taking it in hers. Never in my life did I think an out-of-towner would shake Billy's hand upon first meeting him. Most of the other paranormal inhabitants of Maple Hollow could pass for vaguely human, but certainly not Billy. It had taken weeks for Willow to emerge from her little café. Even now, she was still timid and cautious around some of us. But Harlow, while afraid, was willing to at least try. I didn't know why that endeared her to me so much more, but it did. I was impressed.

"Sweaty palms," Billy said with a chuckle. "But brave."

"Sweating is our family's superpower," Harlow said. "Not as cool as you hulking out, but . . ."

Billy looked at me. "I like this one."

"Yeah." I looked at Harlow, surveying her anew. "I like this one too."

12

HARLOW

We walked around the town square until our ice creams were gone and all that was left were hours of small touches and conversation. I learned about Jordyn's job, her coven, and her life in this town, and I told her about all of my misadventures job-hopping around the world.

Jordyn shivered and broke the now-comfortable silence. "It's getting a bit late. Maybe we should call it a night?"

"Sure." I smiled but internally begged for time to slow down and for the few blocks to Willow's café to become miles long.

It *was* getting late, and I would have to be up before the sun to help open for the morning rush, but more than anything, I wanted to listen to the pretty witch beside me talk about everything under the sun and stars.

We paused in front of Witch's Brew Café, each of us calling the other's bluff. I rocked on the balls of my feet, refusing to be the first to say good night. And lucky for me,

Jordyn spoke first. "When was the last time you went on a date?"

My feet faltered, hovering over the cement for a second, before I took a step forward, continuing to stroll down the sidewalk with my hands clenched in nervous fists in my pockets.

"Does this count as a date?" I peeked at her sideways.

"I mean, I thought it was obvious, but now I'm second-guessing myself," she hedged with a huff of laughter and reddened cheeks.

"No. It's definitely a date, then."

I loved the way she tucked a lock of her glossy brown hair behind her ear when she was nervous. She cleared her throat. "Did you have someone before you moved here?"

We walked through the shadowed gaps between street-lights. They had been designed to look like lanterns and cast the street in a warm orange glow.

"Uh, yeah, back when I was a dog groomer in Springfield."

"You were a dog groomer?"

"Only for a week." I shook my head. "The job didn't stick to me nearly as well as the fur did." That garnered a little chortle from her, and it made me stand a little taller. I liked making her laugh. "One of the girls there and I went out a few times. Nothing serious."

"How long ago was that?" She toyed with her rings like she knew it was an invasive question to ask but couldn't help but ask it anyway.

"About two months ago. When's the last time you went on a date?" I regretted my question the moment it left my lips. Willow had told me that Jordyn had been keeping to herself since her ex had passed, and the tension between us felt thicker than before.

Jordyn didn't immediately answer, but when she did, it was vague. "It's been a long time."

I left it at that. The last thing I wanted to do on a first date was dredge up painful history that I wasn't sure I was supposed to know yet. We passed Midnight Market again, the place now booming with evening locals. Most of the tourists had disappeared the closer it got to midnight, while all of the locals had started coming out of the woodwork. It looked like the cast of every haunted mansion was roaming the streets, but instead of paid actors in makeup, it was real-life monsters, demons, and vampires.

Distant howls filled the air, and I stepped in closer to Jordyn on instinct.

"Don't worry." She clicked her fingers, and a blue flame danced in the palm of her hand. "They'll leave you alone if they don't want to get turned into a corgi."

I gaped at the flame in her palm. "You can do that?"

She weighed her head from side to side with a mischievous smirk. "I could try."

I let out a little snort as I watched the dancing light.

"Here." She held the flame toward me. "Touch it."

I looked at her warily. "I'm not going to burst into a fireball, am I?"

"It hasn't happened yet." She moved her hand closer to me. "But I have a salve for burns, just in case."

She winked, and I held up my hand, nervously moving my fingers closer.

"I'm trusting you," I said.

Her crooked smile widened.

Curse that adorable smile! I relented, brushing my fingertip across the dancing flame. To my surprise, it was cool. My finger prickled, the feeling like Pop Rocks dancing across my skin and up my arm giving me goose bumps.

I looked at Jordyn, the flames dancing in her eyes and glowing on her pale skin. She was so beautiful. I watched intently as her lips parted. My heart thudded, and I was screaming in my head to make a move, but Jordyn lurched into me, her face colliding with mine before we both tumbled backward.

"Oh my goddess, I am so, so, *so* sorry!" She cringed, dusting golden leaves off me and helping me up. "I, uh, tripped!"

"You tripped standing still?" I asked skeptically. "It felt more like someone shoved you into me." I looked over her shoulder but saw nothing but empty street.

"It's definitely a possibility," she gritted out. "Lots of ghouls out at this time of night. We're nearing the witching hour, I think. We should probably get you home. Don't you have to get up like crazy early?"

She was rambling, turning in a circle, looking everywhere but at me.

"Hey." My voice was calm as I grabbed her hand and squeezed. She looked down to where our fingers were joined. "Walk me home?"

"Okay." Her eyes darted around one last time before I tugged her back in the direction we'd come.

Keeping her hand in mine, we wandered back to the twinkling candle in the window of the Witch's Brew. Her delicate fingers felt good in mine, despite mine probably being a bit sweaty. But she didn't seem to mind.

"Two years ago," she said.

"What?"

"My last first date was two years ago."

"Oh," I mused.

"We dated for about a year before we broke up." Jordyn scrunched her eyes closed, and the muscle in her jaw flexed.

"I mean, *I* broke up with her," she corrected. "And she died a few months later and I just haven't gone out with anyone since."

"Oh, I'm so sorry."

She glared over her shoulder. "I'm getting less and less sad about it by the day."

I had no idea what that meant. But I brushed off the odd comment. Grief did weird things to us all, I supposed.

"I can't imagine there's a lot of queer people in a little town like Maple Hollow," I said.

Jordyn shrugged and threw a look around the square. "You'd be surprised. There's a pretty big overlap between the paranormal and rainbow communities."

We walked past a monster with black and purple hair draped across one eye.

"I guess that makes sense," I replied.

The monster flashed us the "rock on" symbol, and we tried desperately to keep ourselves composed as we flashed it back. When he was halfway down the block, we finally burst out laughing, Jordyn's face bright red as she wiped a tear of joy from her eye.

We stopped in front of the burgundy door to the Witch's Brew Café, still smiling at each other.

"This was fun," I said, lingering at the steps.

"Yeah. It was." She smiled back at me. "Maybe we could do it again sometime? Or, er, uh, not show you around again 'cause I obviously just did that, but maybe, like, we could go . . ." She gestured to the café window. "Willow always decorates the windows with carved pumpkins this time of year. Maybe we could go pumpkin picking? Saturday. If you want. No pressure."

Her rambling was so adorable, I couldn't help myself. I stepped in and slowly kissed her on those sweet, soft lips. It was the gentlest of kisses, a little spark that I already knew would eventually set me aflame. But right now, I protected that perfect little ember as she hummed against my lips. I reluctantly took a step back.

Another night. Another night, I would run my hands through her hair and plunder her mouth and taste every sweet inch of her gorgeous body . . . but tonight, I'd leave it at a sweet, little kiss—a question mark—that she could answer when she was ready.

"A pumpkin patch date sounds perfect," I said with a wink, leaving her seemingly stupefied on the sidewalk as I stepped into the café.

13
JORDYN

Lou snickered from behind me as we watched the door to the Witch's Brew close. The embarrassment of almost face-planting into my date's lips still burned even after the amazing kiss we'd just shared. I brought my fingers to my lips to savor the feel of Harlow still lingering there.

"You are so totally fucked!" Lou's voice yanked me back into the moment.

I angrily snapped my fingers at the air beside me, the only indication I'd heard her.

"I know how to pick 'em, don't I?" she gloated, swarming around me like a deranged moth.

I scrubbed a hand down my face and trudged back toward my apartment, all of the delight of the date bleaching from Lou's exuberance as she trotted behind me.

"Although, I thought we'd never see the inside of a building again the way you two were circling the square. You know you live here, right? You know where all the best places are to sit and have a chat."

"Do ghosts ever get tired?"

"That's beside the point."

"Maybe I thought you'd get bored . . . or take a hint. I can't believe you shoved me into her like that." I ignored her critique of the date.

"I wouldn't have had to get involved if you weren't being a coward. She gave you so many openings to make a move and you weren't taking them!"

"Maybe I was taking my time," I countered, reaching the apothecary door and walking through the darkness of the closed-up shop.

"Do you want me haunting you for a decade, Jords?" Lou asked as we trudged up the stairs to the apartment. "I'm helping expedite things."

When I opened the door, Iris was on the couch surrounded by a halo of dusty, old books. She peeked up at me. "Well?"

I looked over at Lou then back at Iris. "One date wasn't the solution, apparently."

"I'm not surprised," Iris grumbled, flipping through her books more frantically. "Going on one date seemed like a weird marker of helping a ghost pass over."

"But why not?" I demanded, pointing an accusatory finger at Lou as she casually strolled around the living room. "I've gone on my date. I'm actively trying to move on. Now you need to move on too."

Lou rolled her eyes. "I'm going to need a little more reassurance that you won't bail on this one for absolutely no reason."

I walked into the small kitchen in the corner and opened the fridge. The apartment had four rooms: the living space, which served as our living room, kitchen, and dining area, two bedrooms, and a bathroom. The benefit was its proximity to work and the rest of the town.

"Oh, I have a reason." I grabbed two bottles of hard cider and brought one to Iris before taking a long swig of my own. "There's a ghost haunting me. That's an excellent reason to hit pause on a relationship."

"Okay, I'm dying to know, how was the date?" Iris fished a coaster from the coffee table drawer and set her cider on it, careful not to spill on the old books strewn across the surface. "Was it fun? Was she cool? She's really hot. I bet it was great. Did you kiss?"

I cut Iris a look as she peppered me with all those questions. "Can we deal with the whole Lou thing first?"

I looked over my shoulder as Lou was steaming her breath on the floor-length mirror in the corner and writing, *They kissed.*

Iris clapped with glee. "Ooh! You *did* kiss!"

"Will you stop!" I shouted at Lou. It was her latest corporeal party trick.

"What's the point in being a ghost if I can't write creepy things in steamy mirrors?"

"I can't believe you kissed. That's huge," Iris said at the exact same time.

All of this talking over each other was breaking my brain.

"It would have been better if Lou hadn't shoved me into her first." I groaned and then glared at Lou. "That push was petty."

Lou folded her arms across her chest. "You weren't complaining when her face was plastered to yours."

"No more interfering," I said. "You can't be around when I'm dating her. It's too distracting. I'm going to scare her off."

"So you're going to keep seeing her?" Lou and Iris chirped together.

Iris's bulging eyes fixed on me. "You're planning a second date already?"

I rubbed my temples with my forefingers, wishing that if I rubbed hard enough, Lou would magically disappear.

I wanted to go on another date with Harlow. She was funny and boisterous and exciting and so ridiculously beautiful. And maybe that thrill that zipped down my spine when I thought of her scared me a little, but witches could handle a little scary, couldn't they?

Lou picked up my cider and twirled it in the air before trying to hand it to me.

Iris perked a brow. "Lou's control over solid objects is getting pretty serious. Which makes me think that you're not doing what you said you were going to do and move on."

"Everything feels so . . . hard," I said. "How can I move on when my ex is literally hanging from lamp posts during my first date in years?"

"I think we're looking at this the wrong way," Iris said. "You're going to have to find a way to ignore her, but more than that, it's not like a date or even two are going to magically make you move on. You have to believe that you're ready to move on and just do what feels good."

"That's easier said than done," I answered, though I knew she was right. I'd been naïve to think that going on one date would help Lou pass back over.

"I know it feels impossible, you've been stuck for so long, but it isn't really up to Lou, you know? Usually, a spirit passing over is for a more definitive thing, like their killer being brought to justice."

I nodded. Hearing that validated something that had

been gnawing at my thoughts. "We should keep looking into that too," I said. "Something there isn't adding up."

"You're really not going to let that go?" Iris knew better than that. "Fine."

"Until then"—I pointed at Lou—"you need to hang back here while I go on the pumpkin patch date."

"You're taking her to the pumpkin patch?" Iris crooned. "That's so adorable! Harlow doesn't happen to have a queer younger sister that you know about, does she?" She frowned down at her books. "I really need a girlfriend."

That was an understatement.

Iris dated often, but in true queer fashion, her exes all knew each other, and the pool of fresh relationships was as dry as a desert. Her last girlfriend had been a werewolf, but the pull of following the moon around the world had been more alluring than dating a witch in a small town.

"I think it's just her and Willow, but maybe another wayward hottie will stumble into town," I offered. "We can do a conjuring spell tonight."

I was only half joking.

"We're not going to *Practical Magic* my love life."

I shrugged. "Why not? It turned out so good for them."

Iris closed the heavy book in her lap and picked up Ichabod. She kissed the top of his head as he aggressively purred and kneaded the air.

"One problem at a time," Iris said in a baby voice to the feline familiar.

I doubted the woman we would summon for Iris would haunt the living daylights out of her, but I was living crazier things thanks to my moment of weakness. Magic made our lives vivid and exciting, but there were plenty of dark pockets that shouldn't be meddled with. Having a séance to say goodbye to your ex-girlfriend had walked that line, and I was *clearly* paying for it.

"Lou can hang here with me while you go on your date. Maybe I can help her remember more of the day she died. Is that okay, Lou?" Iris shouted at the ceiling.

Lou flicked the antique crystal table lamp on the other side of the room, the tinkling bringing Iris's awareness to it. I repressed a snicker. Not all of Lou's games were to annoy me. Some were starting to get on Iris's nerves too.

I gave Iris a sarcastic look. "You thought she would be hovering directly above you?"

"It was worth a shot." She sighed. "Maybe Lou should cat-sit Ichabod for us while we go see Rudy tomorrow too."

"Tell that brat that she's not fooling anyone," Lou said. "I'm not a kid you can dangle a small responsibility in front of and make pleased to be hanging back while you two play Velma and Daphne at the coroner's office." Lou stuck her tongue out at Iris, who was, of course, oblivious.

I shot her a glare. "You overreacted at the police station. It's not farfetched to be worried you'll cause a scene around Rudy."

"I'm not going to turn into a poltergeist," Lou grumbled. "I'm the chillest ghost in all existence, okay?"

"Still," I said, "I don't want you around while Rudy talks about your death."

She gave a long, exasperated sigh. "I'm bored. And do I have to remind you that *I* was the one who may or may not have been murdered?"

Lou picked up a pillow and punted it across the living room like a volleyball. Ichabod dashed after it and landed all four paws on top of it, which sent Lou into a fit of laughter.

"Fine," I said. "You can come along on the investigation, but you cannot come to any more dates. Okay?"

"Alright," Lou said, "but if you mess this date up, I don't want to hear you whining about me hanging around for the next forty years."

The cat merrily hopped back into Iris's waiting lap and demanded tangible affection. Lou lay across the back of the couch and played with a loose lock of red hair at the nape of Iris's neck.

Iris shivered and looked from Ichabod to me. "Lou's sitting right beside me, isn't she?"

"Yep."

"Awesome." Iris clenched her teeth and scooted closer to the armrest on her other side. "You better fall in love with this Harlow chick because your ex is quickly outstaying her welcome."

14

HARLOW

The waitstaff at every café and diner I'd ever eaten at deserved an award and a thank-you note sealed with kitten kisses.

I was sure someone was branding the soles of my feet with a hot poker. My calluses had calluses. My legs felt like jelly.

I made a mental note to ask Jordyn if she had a potion that she was supplying to Willow to keep going day after day. Maybe I could get some too.

The doors had been closed for hours, but I was still finding tasks that needed to be finished before the next morning. I realized that Willow had phases through the day that she used for downtime to prep and clean, but by closing time, there were still heaps of things that had to be done.

Open six days a week. Willow was insane.

Exhausted and aching, I sat cross-legged on my bed with a stack of napkins and a bin of spoons, forks, and knives. I balanced a wet sponge on my knee and used it to close the paper rings that held the little cutlery burrito together.

I looked around my makeshift room. Willow had done a good job turning the space into something more charming than a stockroom. She'd hung moon-covered tapestries across the shelves of saltshakers and bottles of syrup, turning it into a statement wall. The double bed was plush and comfortable with an assortment of Halloween-themed throw pillows she'd clearly bought from the gift shop across the square. A little table sat beside it with a bronze lamp cast to look like a wolf howling at the moon.

The room was cozy, but more importantly, it was free. Maybe I could spruce it up with some knickknacks from around town. I didn't have much from my travels. The one thing I had added was a carved whistle I'd gotten from what was supposed to have been my dream job. Looking at it now hanging on the back of the door, it felt like a lifetime ago.

Willow's apartment upstairs was a one bed, one bath. Whoever had built it hadn't bothered to add a full kitchen since the shop was directly below. But her bathroom had a clawfoot soaking tub, and I couldn't wait to finish bundling silverware so I could fill it with piping-hot water for a long bath.

A tentative knock dashed away my vision of a bubble-filled soak. "Come in," I called out.

Willow opened the door, wearing yoga pants, a tank top, and an open terrycloth robe. Her hair was up in a bun, and she'd clearly just washed her face, given the matching terrycloth headband that held her hair off her face.

She leaned against the doorjamb and looked around the room as if trying to find her words when her eyes landed on the tray of cutlery. "I can get to those in the morning."

"It's fine. I can finish them." I continued wrapping up the parcels.

"Harlow," my sister said, wandering over and perching

at the end of my bed. "I know that what happened with Agnes and the mice were accidents. And I know that you understand that in this town, they were considered major incidents. Aside from them making the township newspaper, they could have really hurt the only thing keeping me afloat."

"I know. I just—"

"Luckily," she continued, a warm, forgiving smile spread over her lips, "we also have a bunch of magic wielders who can help us fix whatever it is we messed up."

I nodded, but the rock in my stomach sank further when I saw that her eyes still held something that felt like pity. "I feel like I'm a bad omen." I dabbed the sponge along the paper ring. "Wherever I go, bad things follow."

"You're not. I know you're not settled yet, but maybe if you stick around long enough, you'll get the hang of this town." Willow grabbed one of the throw pillows and hugged it to her chest. "You know, I had some serious calamities when I first moved here too."

I couldn't imagine my sister messing anything up, even when she was freshly twenty-one and right out of college.

"You nearly kill a vampire?" I asked, perking a brow at her.

"No, not quite." She wrinkled her nose with a chuckle. "Someday, I'll tell you all about the first time I realized that there were real mermaids."

"If you told me now, I would feel less crappy about yesterday," I probed.

"Soon, I promise. This place is so special to me that I sometimes lose sight of things."

"It's amazing, Willow. You should be so proud of all you've achieved here."

"I am." She scooted a little closer and moved the tray

aside. "But I'm now more aware of the reason I never hired anyone to help me. I care a little too much about this place. But having you here and helping take up the slack has shown me that I need to let some things go."

I bridged the distance between us and wrapped her up in a hug. "I'm sorry."

"I'm sorry too. I'm going to try to be less of a hard-ass if you promise to give me a little more time to get used to this new arrangement. Let's go a little easier on each other."

"Deal."

I loved that we could still do this. It was something about having a sister that I loved. No matter how much time had passed, we could still fight, still say the worst things to each other, then still hug it out and move on. I didn't think any other relationship I had was as resilient as the one I had with Willow. I made the intention then to try harder to keep in touch with her when I inevitably moved on to my next adventure.

"By the way, your kitchen banishment has ended," Willow said. "Customers have been asking if I've got you locked up in the cleaning closet, so they must like you. I think they're getting sick of only seeing my face."

I chuckled. "I still feel terrible, so I have a small peace offering, if you're serious about letting go a little."

"I didn't think saying that was going to bite me in the ass already."

"Stop. I'm serious." I pushed at her shoulder playfully. "Jordyn and I are going to the pumpkin patch on Saturday evening, and I want to find you the perfect assortment for your fall decorations."

Willow's face pinched for a second. "Well, you know this town goes all out, so I usually get a couple of small pumpkins and gourds for the tables and then four big ones for the windows and . . . No, you know what?" She smiled at me. "Whatever you pick will be perfect."

I raised my eyebrows at her. "Impressive."

"I'm working on it." She shrugged. "So you and Jordyn, huh? Have I earned my sisterly right to hear about your first date?"

"I don't know. Are you going to spill your guts about you and wolf boy?"

She fussed with the collar of her robe. "There's nothing to tell."

"You're the worst liar," I teased, and she playfully elbowed me before pulling me back into a hug. "You can't keep still, and your ears are rose red."

She knew she was caught. "Don't you *dare* blab my tells to the town. I need to have some secrets."

I held up two fingers in my best impression of Scout's honor, and she rolled her eyes. "I'm glad you're here, Harly. I know I'm not the best at showing it. But I'm really, really glad you're here."

The sincerity bloomed on her cheeks, and I knew that the storm from my first day in Maple Hollow was finally over.

I hugged her so tightly that she groaned. "I'm really glad I'm here too, Wills."

15

JORDYN

Rudy swiveled in his chair, steepling his fingers as he listened to Iris and me explain why we wanted the toxicology report from a death that had taken place over a year ago. His hollow eyes stared at us, his face expressionless. He had the lean, spindly body of a human man, although elongated and stretched out as if his body were made of taffy.

"Something about all of this just isn't right," I pleaded with Rudy. "You knew Lou since she was a baby. Does it really sound like her to get wasted and behind the wheel of a car in the middle of the day?"

Lou sat atop one of the six filing cabinets behind Rudy, swinging her legs through the metal drawers below her.

"I know grief does strange and surprising things to people." Rudy eyed me with accusation.

Well. I assumed he eyed me. He didn't, in fact, have eyeballs.

Rudy had been close to the demon side of Lou's family. He had performed the autopsy, delivered the news to her parents, and had even given a eulogy at her funeral. I didn't blame him for hating me or blaming me for what had happened to Lou.

"I wasn't grieving," Lou protested.

"She wasn't grieving," I echoed, folding my arms over my cable-knit sweater.

If Rudy had eyebrows, I swore he would have arched one. "I've worked in this job long enough to see people do all sorts of surprising things." His voice was an echoey baritone, reverberating around his hollow pumpkin skull. "I *also* know that when people lose someone they care about, they try to make meaning out of things."

I balled my hands into fists and took a step forward. Iris swept in front of me, always covering my bursts of anger.

"How's Sheila doing, Rudy?" Iris asked in a saccharine falsetto. "You know, I've just made a delectable new perfume that, um, really gets the passion going, if you know what I mean."

Rudy's head swiveled toward Iris. It was a poorly kept secret that he and his pumpkin-headed wife were having marital troubles. I had to bite my lips together to keep from smiling. Iris had an innocent face, but she was a witch through and through.

Iris lifted the flap to her leather messenger bag and fished out a vial. She waggled it and then set it on Rudy's desk.

Rudy's gaze dropped to the vial. "I suppose you'll be wanting to barter this toxicity report for it?"

"A gift for a gift," Iris said. "Let poor Jordyn get some closure."

Rudy let out a breathy sigh and turned his chair around to the filing cabinet behind him.

"That sweet little doe is a master of manipulation," Lou

said with an impressed nod. "You hang on to her. Everyone needs a best friend like that."

I smiled down at my shoes, unable to relay the message to Iris aloud.

"Here ya go." Rudy dropped a thin file onto his desk with an unceremonious smack. "I expect that to be returned by this time tomorrow."

"Of course," Iris crooned. "Enjoy the perfume," she added with a wink and grabbed the file.

Lou dropped to the floor. The cabinet she had been perched on wobbled, catching Rudy's attention. Could he see Lou, too? Or maybe feel her the way Iris had? He was the medical examiner in a spooky town; he had to have seen or known ghosts before.

I wasn't given the chance to think on it more, though, because Iris practically shouted, "Have a good night—I mean, day," then hustled me out the door.

We were two buildings down when she started waving the folder in front of her. "Goddess, I was choking on that disinfectant smell. How does that not bother him?"

"He doesn't have a nose," I pointed out. "Here. Let me look."

I grabbed for the file right as a figure came barreling out of the alley. We collided, papers flying everywhere as a familiar voice started saying, "Sorry! Sorry!"

I glanced up from where I was crouched collecting the papers and saw Harlow, who propped a stuffed trash bag against the corner of the building before she joined me to help.

"Harlow!" I squeaked as she passed me a wayward sheet of paper.

"Sorry, I was trying to get the bag in the dumpster. The one behind the bakery was full so I had to hunt for one all

the way over here. I must have swung it a little too forceful-
ly," she said, her cheeks turning a shade of tomato.

I chuckled. "Just a little."

Iris had darted onto the grass to grab the last two sheets of
paper. "Got 'em!" she shouted as she grabbed the last page
from where it clung to the fake cobwebbing around the gazebo.

Harlow looked down at the file in my hands. "A coroner's report? Do I even want to know what witchy ritual
involves medical documents?"

That made a little burble of surprised laughter escape
my lips. "Witchy rituals?"

She waved around the square. "I don't know! It was the
first thing that came to mind."

Goddess, her smile was incredible. It was this shining,
megawatt sort of smile that made my insides light up. It was
like even the ether around her had a shimmer to it.

"Jordyn?" she asked, and I realized I was just gaping at
her aura.

Smooth. I was a total Salome.

I debated lying to her about why I had this folder. It
could've been filed under General Witch Things, but with
the way she was looking at me, I couldn't do it.

"Not this time," I admitted. "We're investigating someone's death." I winced and waited to see how that confes-
sion landed with my hopeful paramour.

Harlow's brows pinched together in concern. "Isn't that
something the police should be doing?"

"The police around here are intentionally sort of lax," I
said with a grimace. "This was someone special to me, and I
just want to make sure nothing suspicious happened."

"Oh," she said. "Is this the ex-girlfriend you were telling
me about?"

"Yeah." My words fell away as Iris came running back, panting and shoving the last page into the file.

"Well, uh, let me know if you need any help with the investigation," Harlow said. "I'm not a very good sleuth, but I can supply the coffee and donuts."

Why did she have to be so adorable?

"Say yes," Lou said, hovering right behind my ear. "Let her help."

I swatted my hand straight through her like I was shooing a fly and turned back to Harlow.

"I just might take you up on that." I smiled and quickly ushered Iris away before I could dig the hole any deeper.

The last thing I needed was to rope Harlow into this side of my madness.

"You should've invited her back to the apothecary," Lou chided. "Kill two birds with one stone and all."

"Would investigating your death count as a date?" The words came out louder than I intended.

"Lou wants Harlow to help investigate her death?" Iris inferred from my muttering.

"No. Lou wants to meddle where she doesn't belong," I answered as we crossed the street.

Lou swam through the air to catch up with us, then walked backward directly in front of me until we got to the doorway of the apothecary.

"The sooner you grow closer to her, the sooner I leave," Lou insisted.

"I don't want to bond over your death," I hissed.

We stepped inside, and I rounded the counter to sit on the stool, then flipped through the pages. There were initial reports by the police that looked more like chicken scratch than words, then a list of results done with a blood and fluid sample. I skimmed to the bottom of the last page and my jaw dropped.

"What?" Lou and Iris asked simultaneously.

I glared down at the paper. It couldn't be right. "There wasn't a drop of alcohol in your blood when you crashed."

"But . . ." Iris came to my side and peered over my shoulder. "Dougall said the car reeked of alcohol?"

"Well, either Dougall's lying or . . ." I frowned down at the papers, then looked up at a stone-faced Lou, who finished my thought, saying, "Or someone else was in the car when it crashed."

16

HARLOW

Willow had warned me that Maple Hollow would be overrun with curious families, social media influencers, and retirees looking for a thrill as the weeks drew closer to Halloween.

Willow spent the morning dashing about, making the coffee orders for Bats & Broomsticks. The bed-and-breakfast, located just behind the haunted orchard, was already fully booked for the season. Willow provided them with their morning coffees while their patrons enjoyed the apple-themed pastries provided by Wyatt. The intricacies of the town ecosystem were both impressive and seamless.

When Wyatt came through the back door at six a.m., he dropped off our usual delivery but lingered near the baked goods case, watching my sister with a glint of pride as she quickly filled her customers' orders.

She finished then turned to him. They both shifted from one foot to the other, their smiles tight but obvious.

"I thought I'd take your hot canisters to the B&B today,"

I heard him say as I reached for a stack of napkins nearby. "Save you the trip?"

Willow looked over her shoulder at me, realizing my shameless eavesdropping. "That's sweet of you, but I can send Harlow over if you have your hands full."

"Oh." Wyatt deflated. "I'll just see you later then."

"Tomorrow, for our fall menu meeting?"

Wyatt answered with a curt nod and dipped his chin to the both of us as he walked out to his truck.

I rolled my eyes and fought the urge to kick my sister for being so dense. It was obvious that they both were interested, but whatever was holding Willow back was going to ruin what could be the real deal.

Before I got a chance to give her crap for brushing Wyatt off, Willow dashed around the corner to help take care of a spill, and I picked up the coffee pot to make the rounds.

While Agnes hadn't returned, I was starting to get acquainted with some of the other locals. And I hadn't accidentally invoked a plague or thrown anyone into toxic shock for two days straight, so things were certainly improving.

"Top up, Billy?" I asked the forest-green patron sitting at the counter. Billy was covered in paint splatters today, the distinct smell of paint thinner wafting off him. Probably giving Midnight Market yet another coat of that glittering onyx. Billy nodded at his plate of pastries, and I glanced up to see a family lingering behind him. "He just clocked out for the night, folks. Photo-ops and free candy corn at Midnight Market later today." I gave the mom a wink. "Don't worry, they open at six p.m., so plenty of time before bedtime."

She smiled at me, put her phone down, and went back to her booth.

"Thank you for that," Billy grumbled into his coffee mug. "I forget how intrusive the tourists are during the busy season." When he was putting on a show, he was the life of the party, but away from the crowd, he was more reserved, and I could tell he had little patience for bullshit.

I huffed a laugh. Billy and I had reached a tentative friendship, with him just as wary of me as I was of him. I had a feeling he was keeping an eye on me on behalf of my sister, or maybe on behalf of the town at large. No more emergency allergy incidents on his watch.

"I don't know how you pull twelve-hour shifts every single night," I said as I stacked saucers. "Or drink three cups of coffee before you go to bed, for that matter."

He hummed around the lip of his mug before he set it down. "I'm not human, remember? My body reacts differently to caffeine."

"Right." I cleared my throat. "I'm still getting used to that."

"Humans often forget that they are not the default. Takes a couple years to realize that you're the odd ones. Willow knows all about that." He dropped some cash on the counter, blotted his mouth, and rose. "Have a good shift, Harlow."

I blinked. It was the first time he'd called me by name. That felt like a victory of some kind, even if it had been meted out with a dose of criticism.

"Have a good sleep, Billy," I called after him as he quickly walked out the back door.

"You have got to tell me what kind of face paint he uses!" I looked up to find a gaggle of teenage girls looking at me. They all had their phones out and were snapping selfies and pictures of their breakfasts.

"It's a Maple Hollow secret, I'm afraid." I winked and they pouted for a moment before turning to one another to gab.

The door jingled open, and I wandered to the register to greet the new patron. It was the slower part of the afternoon, when most people wandered in but lingered for hours before closing time. I'd expected another family coming in for mugs of hot chocolate between the hay bale ride and apple picking, but instead, I found Jordyn.

"Hi." She smiled and swept a lock of hair behind her ear.

"Hi," I replied, shifting my weight back and forth.

Before I could open my mouth to compliment her on the green-velvet dress she was wearing, Willow came out from the kitchen with a box of scones.

"Hey, Jordyn," Willow said, setting the scones on top of the bakery case. "How are you doing today? Keeping busy?"

"No. I mean, um, I'm good. The shop is good. I just . . ." Her eyes pinged between Willow and me.

Willow side-stepped into me. "Harlow, can you take the recycling out for me? It's overflowing." She glanced at Jordyn. "Maybe Jordyn could give you a hand?"

"Sure!" Jordyn brightened as I glowered at my sister.

"Very smooth," I whispered to Willow, who was grinning at me wickedly. "Expect retribution the next time Wyatt is here."

There were two cans in the recycling bin. I picked them both up and passed one to Jordyn, who followed me out the back door.

"Sorry I got you roped into work while you're not actually at work," I told her. "I promise to never let Willow plan a date for us again."

Jordyn chuckled. "Your sister knows about us then?"

I fought the smile pulling my lips up at the way she said "us." As if after one date, we were already a couple. As if there were an "us" after a single kiss.

God, I loved women.

In two more dates, I would be ready to adopt a cat with her.

Instead of professing my love or proposing, I just answered, "She knows."

We wandered down the alley toward the recycling bin at the end of the narrow lane.

Jordyn meandered behind me. "So," she started, "as much fun as lugging empty milk cartons is, I actually came to ask you something."

I perked up at that, little butterflies dancing low in my belly. "Yeah?"

"Um, I'd like to take you up on your offer to help with the investigation? Maybe you'd like to come over tonight and help Iris and me with the scrying?"

I turned to face her. "Scrying?"

"We are going to do a spell, then peer into a silver bowl of water. It's an ancient practice to open our minds and eyes to elements that we may not normally see or feel." She waved her hand as if that statement were boring. "Anyway, we could use some caffeine and sugary treats if you want to come hang out?"

I practically choked on my inhale. "While you do mystical spells to see the past?"

"You know, normal hangout things," she added sarcastically.

My heart did a little flip. "Hell yeah. Count me in."

She had to trust me to invite me to something so personal, right? And if she trusted me, maybe that meant she liked me just as much as I liked her.

I lifted the recycling bin lid so she could toss her can in. It landed with a clink, and I added mine to the pile.

"Is this your way of saying you wanted to see me before our date on Saturday?" I asked.

Saturday felt like an eternity instead of just two days away, and I had been racking my brain for ways to see her before then.

"Maybe it is," she admitted. The giddy gay cheerleader in my chest was doing cartwheels as Jordyn's cheeks dimpled. "In the least clingy, super-casual way possible, I wanted to see you sooner."

A strand of hair fell across her brow, and before she could reach up to tuck it behind her ear like she usually did, I lifted my hand and swept it back myself. Her breath caught, her big eyes searching mine.

"Fuck it," she whispered and shot forward, wrapping one hand around my neck and pulling my face down to meet hers.

Our mouths collided, tongues clashing as I tasted her sweet lips. My hands immediately wrapped around her lean body, pulling her against me and spinning her around to lean against the brick wall until I had her caged in. Fuck, I wanted her so badly, and the way she devoured my mouth made me think she felt exactly the same. Her hips ground into me as my hands roved her curves. So much for slow, sweet kisses. No, I wanted her stripped naked, my skin against her skin, pulling those breathy, little moans from her lips.

I heard a low whistle from behind me, and we pulled apart to see the police chief standing at the end of the alley, his bushy eyebrow arched. The hairs on the back of my neck rose with the sudden urge to shield Jordyn from the asshole ogling us.

"What do you want, Dougall?" Jordyn called to him, her voice laced with venom.

His shoulders shook with a laugh. "Maybe take the love

fest inside there, Jordyn? There are families roaming the streets."

"Why don't you go hump a fire hydrant or something?" Jordyn seethed.

Dougall merely laughed. "As soon as you stop humping your girlfriend in view of the town square, okay, *Sabrina*?"

Heat crept up from below the collar of my shirt.

"Got it, thanks, officer," I interjected, cutting off their spat. The last thing I needed was to be the instigator of a werewolf-witch feud.

Dougall paused on me for a moment but must have decided against pushing the matter any further. He wandered off as I grabbed Jordyn by the wrist and tugged her to face me. "As much as I'd love watching you turn him into a toadstool, I should get back to work."

She sighed but slid her eyes up my body to meet mine. My skin tingled, and the anger and embarrassment from before were washed away.

"I'll see you tonight? Around eight?" Jordyn's voice was deep and raspy and oh-so-sexy. And her gaze was promising something my body was desperate to cash in.

"I'll be there, caffeine and croissants in hand," I said with a nod.

I really wished her roommate wouldn't be there, but maybe a buffer would be a good thing. This witch and I had gone on one single date and I was already ready to jump her bones.

Fuck. Maybe I should book the U-Haul now . . .

17
JORDYN

Harlow knocked on the back door of the apothecary at eight p.m. on the dot, and I had the sneaking suspicion she'd been pacing outside our apartment for the last several minutes. Because when I opened the door, she froze mid-step.

"That was fast," she said, eyeing me. "I thought you lived on the second floor?"

"I was just returning something to the shop," I said quickly as I swept a lock of hair behind my ear. She didn't need to know I'd been leaning against the foyer wall, waiting for the last several minutes.

"You two are disgustingly adorable," Lou said from behind me, and my genuine smile turned into a grimace. I waved a hand behind my back, trying to signal her to fuck off. "Don't you shoo me," Lou grumbled. "I'm not a frickin' pest."

I wanted to say, "Well then stop acting like one," but Harlow was doing that nervous, little shuffle she did when we let the silences between us run a little too long.

Harlow held up a wrinkled white paper bag and a cardboard tray with four to-go cups. "Coffee and muffins?"

"The perfect food for witch work," I said with a laugh. "You look nice," I added and then bit my bottom lip to keep from saying more ridiculous things.

Her hair was still damp, her bangs swept away from her face. I wished I knew how she made comfortable clothing look so damn good. The cuffs of her short-sleeved shirt hugged her biceps just right, and her dark-wash jeans accentuated her curves, making my mouth water.

Harlow blushed. "Thanks, I showered."

"Oh, so that's the secret," I joked. I stepped back to allow her to pass through. "Come on in. We're just about ready."

Harlow followed me up the stairs and into the apartment. She paused just inside the entryway and surveyed the kitchenette, sofa, and TV with a perplexed expression. A twinge of embarrassment ran through me. The apartment wasn't a total mess, but it was well lived in. I hadn't done a single dish in the sink all week and half-empty water glasses sat on several surfaces.

I watched Harlow for another moment, trying to will her thoughts into my head, but that wasn't a magic I possessed. But then her eyes met mine, and without mystical intervention, I knew she wasn't disgusted but pleased. Her small, warm smile filled her eyes and released all the butterflies I'd been holding captive in my belly.

Iris cleared her throat, and Harlow's eyes drifted over to where Iris was sitting at the low coffee table. She'd drawn a salt pentagram and placed white candles at its points, and in the middle was a silver bowl of moon water for gazing into.

"You still okay with this?" I asked Harlow as I took the

coffee and muffins from her and set them on the kitchen countertop.

She shrugged. "I just expected it to be . . . I don't know, less normal? More witchy?"

I winced.

"I mean your apartment. It's very...cozy. I don't really know what I expected, but it's nice."

I released a relieved sigh. At least she hadn't been scared off by the events we had planned.

"We keep the virgin sacrifice altar in the other room," Iris said as she wandered over and selected the cinnamon cappuccino from the tray. She took a sip and hummed. "Thank you for this."

"I—uh . . ." Harlow stared at her, then relaxed when Iris gave her a cheeky wink.

I snickered and wanted nothing more than to lace my fingers with Harlow's. Instead, I took her by the elbow and led her closer to the table.

"Happy to help." Harlow smiled tentatively, waving to the pentagram. "Though I don't know if I'll be of much use for whatever that is."

Iris took out a fist-sized crystal and a town map from the credenza and set them on one corner of the table.

"Okay, I'm starting to pick up the witchy vibes a little more," Harlow joked.

"Have a seat," I offered, suddenly remembering my manners. "Can I take your coat?"

Iris stifled a snort at my awkwardness while Lou outright guffawed.

"Trying to get her to take her clothes off already, Jords?" Lou taunted from the corner.

"I'm not taking her clothes off." As soon as the words left my mouth, I blanched.

Fuck. I'd just said that aloud.

"It was just a friendly, suggestive wink," Iris said, attempting—and failing—to cover for me.

I was certain my face was beet red when I turned to Harlow. "It's just a witch thing."

Harlow squinted at me for a second but then passed me her coat without comment. She took a seat across the table from Iris.

I plated up the muffins and brought them over with the rest of the drinks. "There's an extra coffee?" I asked as I set the baked goods on the table next to the knuckle bones.

"Oh yeah," Harlow said as she sipped her double espresso. "One time you came into the café and ordered a soy flat white, another time a skim milk mocha, so I wasn't sure what you wanted. So I made both."

That little gesture made my stomach do somersaults, but I only had a split second to revel in the sweetness before Lou crooned, "I bet she's a lavender oat milk latte kinda gal."

"I'll probably end up drinking them both," I said with a feigned laugh and sat beside Harlow.

"Muffins and moon water." Harlow shook her head. "Sounds like a cute and cozy rom-com."

Iris chuckled. "Welcome to Maple Hollow."

"Ready?" I asked Iris, and she nodded.

Iris closed her eyes and began the spell, her hand hovering over the surface of the water to set her intentions. The pentagram of candles flickered, and I noticed how Harlow scooted closer to me. I dropped my hand under the table and gave her knee a quick, reassuring squeeze before taking Iris's hands across the table.

Carefully, so as not to set my sleeve alight, I gripped Iris's hands tightly and repeated the Latin phrasing. Lou drifted over and sat in the empty fourth seat, her eyes warily holding mine for a second before I screwed them shut to focus. The short incantation filled my ears and sent warmth through my body before heating my fingertips in Iris's palm. We asked the spirits to guide us on the path to truth. I pictured the question in my mind and prayed for an answer: was Lou murdered?

If the water remained clear and unmoving, then the answer was no and that would be the end of it. No more maps, no more spells, no more investigation. But if the water became clouded and started moving, then our suspicions were correct and Lou's death was more nefarious than it had first seemed.

I wasn't sure which answer would bring Lou or me peace.

Harlow shifted next to me. The room went silent, and we all stared into the bowl. Long moments passed, and I worried my eyes were playing tricks on me. A glimmer of light rippled across the surface, and the water became opaque. My stomach flipped, and the hairs on the back of my neck stood straight.

"Shit," Iris hissed.

"Fuck," Lou echoed with her own string of curses.

"What?" Harlow's eyes flared as she looked between Iris and me. "What does it mean?"

I sighed, grabbing the crystal and map that Iris had brought out earlier. I spread the map in front of me. Then, placing the crystal at the center, right on top of the gazebo, I took a deep breath.

I glanced at Harlow. "It means Lou was murdered."

Harlow gasped.

I couldn't imagine how panicked she must feel. This had to be a lot for her, especially during her first few weeks in town. Iris and I did this kind of witchcraft all the time.

We were constantly walking the line between life and death. Hell, we were well-acquainted friends of the afterlife and all things supernatural, but for Harlow, she probably thought she was smack-dab in the middle of a horror movie.

Who expects someone to help solve a paranormal murder after one date? I was rethinking inviting her, but then she took my hand in hers. Our fingers interlocked and squeezed.

"What is she doing?" Harlow studied Iris as the redhead placed her hand on the large crystal and hummed.

"She's asking the Goddess to help us pinpoint the killer's location," I whispered, not wanting to break Iris's focus.

"Right," Harlow whispered back. "Of course she is."

Wind whipped through the air, conjured by the magic, despite us not having a single window open. Iris's eyes flared white, her head pointing skyward as her hand jutted out for a finger to curl a small corner off the town map.

"Holy shit," Harlow whispered as the knuckle bones finally stopped moving. She shuffled over to me, tucking into my side, and I couldn't help myself. I leaned over and kissed her temple.

"It's okay," I murmured. "You're safe."

Harlow's blue eyes locked with mine, and I found myself swimming in their depths. Goddess, those eyes weren't only arrestingly beautiful. I swore they had a spark of magic to them too. It was as if she could see straight into my mind and see all of my jumbled thoughts.

Iris cleared her throat, breaking the spell that held me in Harlow's gaze. I turned to my friend, and she blinked, the magic fading from her eyes. "Are you thinking what I'm thinking?"

I was already standing, breaking my grip with Harlow's hand with an apologetic squeeze. Grabbing one of the candles from the pentagon, I held it sideways and waited for the wax to start to drip.

"What are you thinking?" Harlow's voice had a slight wobble to it.

"Ask again," I said.

"Do you think . . ." Harlow's gaze found mine. "Do you think the killer is in Maple Hollow?"

"Is that why I was coming back here?" Lou asked. "Or do you think the asshole who killed me was driving me back here for some reason?"

"I don't know," I replied, my answer being equally given to Lou and Harlow.

Iris took a deep breath and started chanting again. When she stopped, the bits of melted wax slithered across the map, collecting slowly to form a circle in the center of the town square.

Harlow made a strangled sound. "The gazebo again?"

"So the killer is here," Iris whispered, shaking her head. "In the gazebo. Right. Now."

"Come on, then!" Lou jumped to her feet. "We've got to go confront the bastard. Maybe he's still there."

Together, the rest of us rose without speaking, all of us seeming to think the same thing. We thundered down the back stairwell and burst into the apothecary. Huddling around the window, we peered out into the town square, which was bustling with tourists and locals. But no one stood in the gazebo.

"Quick." I threw open the front door and hustled onto the sidewalk. "Write down everyone we see," I commanded Iris, who produced a pen and notepad from her back pocket.

Our eyes scoured the town green. Billy Bacchus was taking photos with tourists outside Midnight Market. Willow was sweeping the café's stoop. Wyatt was carrying four giant white boxes of pastries down the street. Dougall McCleighton was eating a candied apple on the bench outside Luna's Hairdresser, probably waiting for his weekly cut. And the local pumpkin patch owner—and swamp monster—Juniper Becker was carting crates of pumpkins on a dolly.

Harlow pointed to a shadowed corner beside the Cauldron Candle Shop. "Who's that talking with Agnes?"

I narrowed my eyes, staring perpendicularly from where the apothecary sat. I had to lift up on my tiptoes to get a clear vantage point. Agnes clutched a black lace shawl to her chest, her head inclined to whisper to a woman with a slicked-back haircut and wearing a perfectly pressed suit.

"That's Ramona Henry," I murmured.

Ramona threw her head back in laughter, though we were too far to hear the sound. She had a presence about her that even strangers seemed to feel. The crowd parted to give the two women a wide berth.

"Since when are the vampires and demons being all chatty?" Iris asked.

"She's a demon?" Harlow squeaked beside me. I wrapped my arm around her waist and tugged her to me.

"Something about this isn't stacking up," I said with a shake of my head. "I think tomorrow night, we should pay old Ramona a visit."

"Can I come?" Harlow asked.

I looked at her, my eyebrows shooting up. "I don't know if that's a good idea. Ramona is . . . well, she's a high-ranking demon—and dangerous, especially to people she doesn't know."

Harlow rolled her shoulders back and extracted herself from my grip. It was adorable watching her try to puff herself up with confidence. "I'll be fine. If I'm with you and

Iris, I'll be safe, and I want to be sure nothing happens to you."

I couldn't help my smile. Maybe she could protect me through sheer determination alone.

"I'm going to let you two say good night." Iris waved her arms around her as she awkwardly added, "And I invite any other spirits gathered on the street to also give you some privacy."

Lou snorted. "Okay, fine."

"Thanks, Iris," I said, flashing her a quick thumbs-up to let her know that Lou was following her inside.

Harlow chuckled. "So I'll see you tomorrow night?"

I nodded, those damned butterflies dancing low in my belly again. "See you then."

Harlow bracketed my face with her hands and pulled me into a scorching kiss. One so hot and torturous that it made me desperate to get somewhere far more private. The ache between my thighs was building when she pulled away and looked into my eyes.

"See you tomorrow, Detective Jordyn." She gave me one last wink before she sauntered down the street.

And I watched her walk *all* the way back to the café before I finally went back inside to have an ice-cold shower.

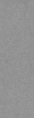

18

HARLOW

The next morning, every booth was crammed full and there was a line out the café door. Willow had me set up the outdoor chairs and tables that she normally reserved for the summer crowd, and each one was immediately occupied despite the chilly breeze. Billy had some choice words about town ordinances for her, but he eventually let the matter go when she reminded him that it was all for the good of the town's economy.

I was taking care of the local fishmonger, Katie, at the till when I heard the back door open.

I repeated her order and set the cup down on the pickup counter. "One large iced matcha latte with oat milk and lavender whipped cream." The thick green liquid mixed with the light purple foam on top.

"Thanks." Katie placed a lid on the cup and swirled her drink around until tendrils of lavender sank into the depths of grassy green. "Looks a little swampy when it mixes, but it's my favorite combo." She reached into the pocket of her thick coat for a few damp bills to drop into the tip jar.

"The other day, I was playing around with the syrups and coffee," I said. "Looked like puke, but it was the best orange, peanut butter, white mocha with almond milk I've ever had."

"Uh, I don't think I'm brave enough to try that one out."

I laughed and grabbed a milk pitcher to clean out. "I was more bored than brave."

"I can see that." She smiled and stepped away from the counter, drink already pressed to her lips.

If more people in this town were like Katie, maybe I could actually make some friends. Katie was one of the few fellow humans who resided in Maple Hollow, but everyone seemed to like her even though she was a little bit strange. But aside from the fish smell, I couldn't put my finger on why. Of course, in this town, that could be said about me too.

"Hey, Mini-Miller," a familiar voice called from behind me.

I turned to see Wyatt walking in with a box of baked goods. I wanted to point out that there was nothing "mini" about me, but seeing as I was the younger Miller sister, the nickname had stuck.

I glanced at Willow through the front window. An elderly couple had stalled her, asking questions that I could tell by the strained look on her face would be easily answered with a quick internet search or a trip to the information booth in the town square.

"It calms down a lot after Halloween," Wyatt said, following my line of sight. "A few more weeks and the rush will be over. Everyone will head off to one of those Christmas-y towns."

"Are those towns like this one?" I perked a brow at him and noted the curl of his lips. "Don't tell me there's a real

Santa Claus too. I'm not sure what to believe at this point."

"Maybe you'll find out someday." Wyatt leaned against the counter, and I decided that was a discussion for another day.

I opened the box he'd brought and surveyed the contents inside: cinnamon rolls, macarons, muffins, scones, and an assortment of puff pastries. He'd also included little sticky notes that listed each baked good's name and any allergies. It struck me how off-theme these foods were for a town like Maple Hollow.

"Hey, Wyatt?"

He jolted like I'd snuck up on him. He'd gotten lost gawking at Willow . . . again. "Yeah, mini?"

"Why aren't any of these pastries Halloween themed?" I waved to the assortment of food. "I mean, they're fall flavored for sure—caramel apple, cinnamon, pumpkin spice —but this place is called Witch's Brew Café, you know? There should be more whimsy!"

He gave me a wary look. "I know," he hedged.

"Maybe you could make some witch-hat sugar cookies or some cauldron-shaped macarons?"

"I could whip them up no problem, but . . ." He scratched the back of his head.

"Let's do it!" I said eagerly. "Black macarons with green and purple buttercream centers."

He glanced back out the window. "We really ought to ask Willow."

"I'm sure she'd be fine with it," I assured him as I used a pair of tongs to line up the cinnamon rolls in the cabinet.

He arched his brow and cocked his head, making him all the more wolflike. "Have you *met* your sister?"

I huffed. "Just add them to tomorrow's delivery," I

pleaded. "Or whenever you can. We'll work her up to the idea one sweet treat at a time."

"Okay." He shook his head. "But it's on your head if she's pissed—"

"I'm good with that," I insisted. Things were always my fault anyway.

This idea could really step things up a notch for her. I stared around the packed room—not that her business was struggling or anything. The café was cute, but there was nothing particularly Instagram-able or witchy about the place other than the coatrack.

My eyes landed on Agnes outside the bay windows. She sneered at the place as if she were cursing it and then kept walking. Not a single vampire had stepped foot in the café since I'd nearly poisoned her with nutmeg. I wondered if that had been the topic of her and Ramona's conversation last night. Maybe they were joining forces to boycott the café. Maybe they'd turn the whole town against us . . .

I whirled to face Wyatt, who was making himself a complimentary cinnamon dulce latte. Usually, Willow made it for him, and I always noted the extra care she put into crafting his drink, but Wyatt knew how to work an espresso machine too.

"Do you know Ramona Henry?"

"The demon?" Wyatt asked with suspicion.

I waited until he stopped frothing his milk and the whine of the steamer died down to speak. "Yeah. Do you know much about her?"

Wyatt's shoulders rose then fell when he turned back to face me. "She's been here forever. She looks young, but she's as immortal as a vampire. I think she owns quite a few souls."

"Souls?" I nearly dropped the scone from the tongs.

"You know—demons, souls. She makes deals for the big guy downstairs." Wyatt pointed to the ground.

"The devil?" I shrieked, and a bunch of heads turned.

I feigned a smile and tried to look busy until the attention was no longer on me.

"Welcome to Maple Hollow." He brought his cup up to his lips and took a sip.

"Always something new," I said anxiously.

"What's your interest in Ramona? You're not planning on selling off your firstborn for wealth or luck, are you?"

"Oh." I waved his question away. "Nothing. I'm just helping Jordyn with something."

Wyatt blew on his coffee. "What does Jordyn want with Ramona?"

I considered spilling the beans, telling him everything about Jordyn's ex-girlfriend and her death and the scrying and the gazebo . . .

Wyatt watched me with quiet amusement. I could probably trust him. He had a very trustworthy face, and he was clearly in love with my sister . . . but it tended to be the sweetest, most innocent guys who turned out to be the murderers in these sorts of situations, and he'd been in the square last night, which *technically* made him a suspect.

Willow arrived just in time to save me from an awkward explanation. "Hey!" Her voice was an octave higher and far cheerier than it had been when she'd left.

"Hey, Willow," Wyatt said back just as sweetly, and I wanted to gag.

Like seriously, I was pretty sure the truck driver at the counter could tell these two had the hots for each other. It was just so painfully obvious to everyone but them.

"I made myself a coffee, didn't want to interrupt your

busy day." Wyatt lifted his mug as if in evidence. "You make it better though."

"I can make you another one?" Willow offered almost too eagerly.

I rolled my eyes, and she elbowed me hard in the ribs.

"Nah, that's okay," Wyatt said. "Next time." He gave Willow a wink, and I swore she made a sound like a pig snuffling for truffles. "See you tomorrow."

"See you!" she exclaimed a little too loudly and waved goodbye.

She waited until he left and then twisted toward me, pointing an accusatory finger. "Say one word and I'll put you back on kitchen duty."

I zipped my lips and wandered off, humming a song from *Lady and the Tramp* as I went.

19
JORDYN

"It's not weird. Just go inside." Lou peeked through the window of the café, her head sectioned by the glass. "It looks like there's a lull. Don't be a chicken."

I had the sudden urge to cluck just to spite her. It was stupid to feel so nervous just walking into the coffee shop and ordering a drink to go. But Harlow had had all night and morning to think about the scrying she'd witnessed. A gnawing feeling in my gut was starting to make me believe that it was too much for her. That *I* was too much for her.

"If you don't go in there, I'm going to throw a brick through this window," Lou threatened with a scowl.

"Vandalizing private property? You wouldn't dare."

Lou stubbornly searched for a loose brick. "Bet."

"Fine! I'm going," I whispered. The last thing I needed was to be written up for property damage.

But I'd only taken two steps before a too-sweet voice called my name. "Jordyn! What are you doing here?"

Katie's big green eyes zeroed in on me.

I should have known it was her by the smell, but today

there was a hint of lavender from the drink she was absent-mindedly slogging about.

"Oh." I stumbled over the word, looking from her to the café door and back. "Just grabbing a coffee on my break."

Her head tilted slightly, but her bright smile didn't fade. "Funny. I thought you said you don't drink coffee?"

Did I ever say that?

"I've developed a taste for it," I replied with a feigned smile. "Tea just doesn't have the same kick it used to."

Her nose scrunched and she let out a squeal of laughter. "You're hilarious."

"Is she for real?" Lou stepped around Katie, evaluating her like some sort of anomaly. "That wasn't even clever."

"Are you ready for the Halloween Festival? You always look so pretty in your ceremonial dresses." A dreamy look smoothed her smile lines.

"Goddess, does every girl in this town have a boner for you?" Lou snarked. "You've got even the fishmonger all doe-eyed."

I ignored the ghostly snipe and said to Katie, "The Halloween Festival is more for the tourists than the coven, but I guess it's fun to dress up."

The bell from the café door sounded behind Katie, and Billy's lumbering form emerged. He spotted Katie first, then slid his gray eyes to me.

"Morning, ladies." His gravelly voice was low and sleepy.

"Hey, Billy," I answered.

"Good morning." Katie took a step toward me, and a new smell hit my nose.

My hand shot up to cover the lower half of my face before I had the sense to stop it. I let out a cough to try and play it off as an allergy, but it was too late.

Billy quirked a brow. "It's a bit early in the morning for liquor, isn't it, Katie?"

"It's the sanitizer," Katie quipped, her cheeks bright red while she fussed with the red bandana tied tight around the crown of her head. She turned to me. "Gotta stay clean in my line of work. Food safety standards and all. One sick day and the whole system is a mess."

"Right," I agreed, but the pity in my tone was glaring.

Lou waved to catch my attention, then pointed toward Billy's shoes. They were covered in fresh red paint.

"Doing some home improvements?" I asked, pointing my chin at him.

"I was helping with the orchard's haunted hayride figures," he said matter-of-factly. "You know Bishop has to repaint them every year around this time. His biggest attraction is the photo area with the big apples that folks shove their heads into. Silly, but humans like what they like." He eyed Katie pointedly; she was the only human in this conversation.

"No, I didn't realize he had to paint them every year," I replied.

Lou's eyes widened as if a memory had hit her.

"Being the mayor, you have to know all the inner workings of the local businesses, Jordyn. Like when the local apothecary owner seems to be leaving her shop midmorning for a pick-me-up. You're not getting into trouble, are you?"

His accusation sent heat up my neck.

"Just wanted a pumpkin-spice mocha to get into the holiday spirit." I plastered on a smile and excused myself.

I slipped between Katie and Billy to hurry into the café. Willow was still nowhere to be seen, but Harlow was at the counter stocking oversized mugs on the shelf next to the espresso machine.

A ghostly hand hit the middle of my back and sent me stepping forward. Harlow's eyes met mine, and her face lit up.

"Um, hi." I cautiously approached the counter and laid my hands on it to have something solid to hold me down to earth.

"Hi."

Was that relief on her face? Excitement? She seemed happy to see me. Or was I misreading this whole thing?

"I was just walking by and thought I'd stop in for a coffee."

"Cool." She smiled. *Curse me, that smile!* "Where are you headed?"

"Nowhere . . . the market . . . we're out of eggs." *Goddess, Jordyn, get it together.*

"The apothecary sells eggs?" She lifted a takeaway cup up and paused with her pen over it.

"Eggshells," I amended quickly. "For protection spells and kitchen magic."

Harlow chuckled. "Like, you can make a cake to ward off bad spirits?"

"Or fertility," I replied and felt the immediate embarrassment.

"Didn't expect that." She pursed her lips. "So what can I make for you?"

"A pumpkin-spice mocha, soy milk, large, please."

"I need to start making these in vats. They're the town favorite today." Harlow gave me another of those beaming smiles, then she turned toward the machines and started the bean grinder.

"In a way, they're also for protection," I said loud enough to be heard over the noise.

Lou snickered from where she'd perched herself on the counter. "You're really nerding out right now?"

"Really?" Harlow's head popped up. "How?"

"Well, cinnamon, clove, and ginger are used to ward off evil. At the beginning of the month, it's customary to blow cinnamon across the threshold of your home for good luck and protection."

Harlow poured the warmed soy milk into my cup and dashed some extra spice mix over the foam before placing the lid on top.

"I like that. Cinnamon is one of my favorite flavors." Harlow nodded and held out the mocha for me. "Maybe I should shake some on my shoulders before we go out tonight?"

"Cinnamon is useless at repelling demons. But Iris and I will protect you."

The corner of her lips pulled into a smile. "I know I'm safe with you."

Goo. My insides puddled into mush at the sultry look in her eye.

"That was smooth," Lou chimed in, breaking the daydream of holding Harlow close.

"I better get going," I told Harlow. "See you tonight?"

"Can't wait."

My stomach flipped as I walked back out to the sidewalk, and the sun shined a little brighter on my way back to the apothecary. But Lou started in on a rant once I closed the door.

"Did you see the paint on Billy's shoes? It's the paint I saw the day I died, the exact shade of red." She paced the length of the store, not bothering to avoid the tables or merchandise.

"Billy isn't the only person who goes to help at the orchard this time of year. And why would Billy kill you?" I answered just in time for Iris to walk out of the storeroom.

"Who did Billy kill?" she asked, searching the room for the ranting ghost.

"Lou saw paint on his boots and now thinks our mayor is a murderous monster." I sighed, planting my butt on the chair next to the register.

"That's terribly offensive to say about his kind," Iris deadpanned. "They're actually the least bloodthirsty of our lot. Did you bring me back anything?"

"Crap. I'm sorry. I forgot."

Iris rolled her eyes and snatched the cup from my hands. "That's okay. I'll just take this one since you *hate* pumpkin spice."

I liked it when Harlow made it, but I wasn't going to win that argument. Nothing was more coveted to Iris than coffee at this hour.

Lou waved her arms about. "Hello! I just found my murderer here!"

"If Billy is on your list of suspects, then we'll check him out after we go see Ramona. She'll know if the elected official was part of your demise."

"Yeah, right," Lou snapped. "The only thing the demon is going to do is offer to snatch your witchling soul in exchange for vague information."

She didn't wait for my comeback. Instead, she slipped through the wall to the storeroom to pout for the rest of the day.

20

JORDYN

I ris and I waited on the steps of the gazebo for Harlow to close up the café for the night. I was second-guessing the choice to bring her to talk with Ramona, but Harlow had insisted, and with two witches flanking her, the demon should behave herself.

Iris's shoulder shook against mine as we huddled next to each other. The bracing wind was extra cutting, the air filled with pinpricks of icy mist. It was the perfect weather for a town like ours.

"Do you think tagging along to meet with a demon is the best idea for a ghost?" I muttered to Lou. She sat behind us, adding to the evening's gloom.

Iris had gotten used to my one-sided conversations but answered anyway, "Uh, hello, she's been murdered. Clearly, a demon will be able to help us figure out what happened."

"What she said." Lou sighed as she stretched her neck from side to side. "Besides, now I have things keeping me here."

Did ghosts get sore muscles?

"I'm moving on, so that's not a reason anymore," I told Lou. "We've been on one official date. We've kissed, *multiple* times. Not to mention all the witchcraft she's witnessed since meeting us. Those are big signs that I'm moving on. I promise I'm over you!"

"Okay, jeez," Lou balked. "Don't need to rub it in."

"Sorry, I'm just . . . worried."

Lou sighed again. "You know what helps with a worried mind? Sex."

I choked on air, letting out a garbled half cough, half gasp.

Iris clapped me on the back. "What did she say?"

"Lou just said I should have sex," I rasped, coughing into my elbow. "You cannot be serious."

"Oh, come on, don't be a prude." Lou let out a light chuckle. "There's nothing more definitive in a relationship than the first big O."

"Please don't let that be the thing that makes you pass over." I pinched the bridge of my nose and looked at Iris. "Be grateful you can't hear what she's saying."

Iris chuckled. "I mean . . . it wouldn't hurt to have a little bit of witchy fun time with Harlow, would it?"

I glared at Iris. "Not you too. We *just* met. Give me like, a whole week to get to know her before I jump into bed with her, okay?"

Iris shrugged. "I just think it might be time to clear the pipes is all."

I hooked a thumb over my shoulder. "I don't need my ghost of an ex watching me fuck my potential new girlfriend—"

"Sorry!" Harlow called from across the square as she dashed toward the gazebo. "I accidentally spilled a salt-shaker, and I didn't want to add an ant problem to the rodent infestation so I had to clean it up." She paused when a cluster of tourists wandered past, adding loudly, "A rodent problem that has been dealt with and no longer exists!"

I tried and failed to hold in my chuckle. I loved when she acted like a chaotic bull in a china shop.

Iris stood and rubbed her hands together, blowing her steaming breath onto them. "Let's get this over with. It's colder than a witch's tit out here." Harlow laughed, and Iris looked at her. "Only we are allowed to make that joke."

"Noted," Harlow said with a smile.

Iris smirked, wrapped her scarf tighter around her neck, and adjusted her red wool coat around her body. I was glad to have Harlow here to keep me somewhat warm on the way to Ramona's place. It wasn't too far of a walk, but like all marches toward enemy territory, it was daunting.

Harlow and I held hands as we followed Iris, who walked at a determined clip through the south end of town. The streets were quieter here as they were off the main thoroughfare. Many of the residents who'd lived here since Maple Hollow was settled lived in the large, older homes that bracketed the street. The white picket fences, old elms, and perfectly trimmed lawns were proof of the pride they took in the town.

The old colonial I grew up in was just around the block from here. I wondered if my mother was at home. Or maybe she was hosting the grimoire club this week and some of the other coven members were visiting for a spell and a drink.

I thought of stopping by to ask if she had any more of those protection necklaces hanging around. I wore mine every single day and could probably make one for Harlow, but my mother was more powerful. I would ask her for one at the next coven meeting . . . and for her to help me cast an additional protection spell over the human holding my hand.

We twisted and twined our way through the neighborhoods until we reached the last row of houses that abutted the haunted forest. The third house down was painted all in black, a lone lantern flickering above the mailbox but not a single shimmer of light inside. I wondered if Ramona even spent any time in her house. I was pretty sure she'd spelled the front door so that when someone knocked on it, she was summoned from hell. Such a twenty-first-century woman—no more crossroads, no more spyglasses. She was one step away from doing deals via text message.

We stopped at the mouth of the walkway that led to the front door. The three floors overhead loomed over us like a black hole. The siding of the house was so matte, so dark that it seemed to absorb all light and color. Otherworldly, just like Ramona.

I felt a bead of sweat slip down my spine despite the frigid night.

Behind me, Lou hummed her disapproval. "Maybe this was a bad idea."

Clearing my throat, I opened my mouth to make a generalized statement about coming back during the day, but Iris strode up to Ramona's door without glancing back to see us rushing up behind her.

The door opened before she even knocked, and out stepped Ramona with a cocky grin. She looked like she was on the cusp of thirty—had looked that way for my entire life. She hadn't a single deep line or gray hair. We all knew this was just her meat suit of choice, and of course, she'd picked one that was shaped like a Greek goddess.

Her cool silver eyes slid from Iris, to me, to Harlow, and then to Lou.

Fuck.

Could she see Lou? Of course, she could. She was a soul trader, after all. Shit. I hadn't thought that through.

Ramona must've read my mind. Her silver eyes slid back to me and then to where my hand was joined with Harlow's. I quickly pulled away, but it was too late. Ramona had seen it.

"I'm guessing you're here about . . ." She looked at Lou with a questioning gaze.

"Lou," Lou supplied bitterly.

Ramona had known Lou for her entire life and hadn't deigned to remember her name.

"Lou," Ramona echoed.

"Wow," Harlow whispered. "She's like a mind reader or something."

Ramona's grin was predatory, and I had the terrible urge to step in front of Harlow to shield her from that look in the demon's eyes.

"I just can see more clearly than most," Ramona purred, inspecting her fingernails. "Now, what do you want to ask me, witchlings?"

A twinge of anger brushed up my neck. *Witchling.* As if we were children. As if Iris and I weren't in line to become our coven's next generation of healers.

"Why were you talking to Agnes in the square last night?" Iris asked.

"You spying on me, Iris?" Ramona spoke in a deep, smooth baritone. *Of course, she remembered only Iris's name.* "Ready to play with someone with a bit more bite?"

I swallowed the growl building in my throat. Iris was gorgeous, and she'd been turning heads all of her adult life. Pretty much every creature in Maple Hollow wanted to get in her pants. But hearing Ramona insinuate that she also wanted a piece of my friend gnawed at my nerves.

Iris folded her arms across her chest. "You are avoiding my question."

"I'm not in the habit of answering questions for free." Ramona's eyes fell to Iris's mouth.

"What do you want, then?" I spoke up, trying to hide the shake in my voice. "We haven't come to barter in souls or time."

"I see." Ramona's grin widened. "Though it would seem that you already have too many souls on your hands anyway."

"What does that mean?" Harlow whispered to me, but I only shook my head in response. Now was definitely not the time to explain that the ex-girlfriend, whose murder we were investigating, was actually a ghost standing behind us.

"I'll take a pound of gold dust for it," Ramona suggested.

"A *pound*?" Iris balked. "Absolutely not."

Ramona shrugged. "Then no answers."

"What would you want with that much gold dust anyway?" Iris pushed.

"Would you like to pay for that question as well?" Ramona countered. Iris balled her hands into fists, and Ramona chuckled. "You've always been feisty."

Iris looked like she was about to lunge at Ramona and show her just how feisty she could be.

"Fine. An ounce of gold dust. And you"—Ramona pointed to Iris—"have to go on a date with me."

Iris's mouth fell open, but neither did she protest.

"Absolutely not," I cut in. "Nope. Not happening, Ramona. Have a good night." I steered Harlow away, pushing her back toward the street. "Iris, come on."

"How about you let your friend answer for herself, hmm?" Ramona rumbled. "What do you say, darling?"

I turned to see Ramona take a step closer to Iris. Ramona stood over a head taller, so Iris had to look up into the demon's eyes, but her firm stance didn't waver.

"Iris?" I called.

"One date," Iris finally answered, and I practically fell over standing still. "At a location and time of my choosing."

"You're a sharp one, witchling." Ramona smiled with sly delight. "At a location and time of your choosing, so long as it is within a year from this night."

"Fine." Iris held her hand out to shake on it.

"Oh, little witch, you know that's not how I seal deals." Ramona tugged on Iris's outstretched hand, pulling Iris in before dropping her head for a kiss.

"Holy shit," Harlow whispered.

Lou whistled low. "Now, *that* is a thorough fucking kissing. Not that your girl seems to mind."

Ramona finally released Iris, who stumbled back, wide-eyed and dazed. Though she also looked surprisingly satisfied with this sudden turn of events.

I grabbed Iris by the crook of her elbow and shoved her behind me. "You're like a fucking doe in the headlights. Stay with Harlow. And stop kissing demons." I turned to Ramona. "Deal's been struck. Spill."

Ramona sighed and thrust her hands into her trouser pockets. "Agnes is brokering an alliance with the demons."

"An alliance about what?" I asked, and Ramona raised her eyebrows like she was going to demand another deal. "I think that kiss was worth a few more questions, don't you?"

She snickered. "The vampires already have most of the monster clans on board. The demons will be next. Witches

153

and wolves probably will come last as you're the most . . . humanlike."

She sneered at the description.

"On board with what?" Iris asked from behind me, and I watched Ramona's ears perk at the sound.

"They want to make Maple Hollow exclusively for paranormal residents." Ramona's silver gaze found Harlow. "They say too many humans are making this town their home nowadays. Soon, it won't be safe for us here."

"Is this about the nutmeg?" Harlow groaned. "I told her I was sorry."

"I, for one, found that quite amusing." Ramona chuckled. "But, yes, you and your sister are certainly part of this equation."

"That is ridiculous," I spat. "Humans have always lived here alongside us."

Ramona pursed her lips, her eyes perusing Iris's figure again before returning to me. "If you want to know their reasons, talk to them. But that's not really why you came here, is it?"

Lou took a step forward. "Did you have anything to do with my death?"

"No," Ramona said boredly and, as far as I could tell, truthfully.

Murder wasn't the demons' repertoire, especially if a soul wasn't on the line for them to take.

"Then who did?" Lou pushed.

Ramona shrugged. "That's for you to find out."

"Who is she talking to?" Harlow whispered to Iris behind me.

"It's a demon thing," Iris whispered back.

We were going to need to start coming up with better

lies about this stuff. Not everything could be explained as a demon/witch/wolf thing.

"Is Lou's death associated with this alliance at all?" I asked, trying to save the situation.

"Hmm," Ramona mused. "Now that is a very interesting question. But I think I've told you enough." She looked at Iris. "Unless you would like to trade for another kiss?"

By the goddess, Iris took a step forward, but I intervened. "Nope! That is enough questions for tonight, thanks, Ramona."

I grabbed Iris's elbow with one hand and Harlow's with the other and steered everyone away like a mother dragging her children out of a candy store.

"Looking forward to that date," Ramona called as I pulled Iris into the night.

After dropping Harlow off in front of the café, Iris, Lou, and I made our way back home. Harlow and I would be seeing each other again soon, but we needed to confront the vampires about this alliance, and taking a willing human into the vampire's lair was a no-go.

"We should go now," Iris said as soon as we were out of earshot of Harlow. "Before Ramona has a chance to warn them that we're on to them."

I linked my arms with her and pulled her in close. "She could have literally materialized into one of their coffins within seconds of us leaving. And we aren't prepared for that."

"Do you really think my death was part of the vampires'

plans," Lou contemplated on my other side. "It's been a year. What would they have been waiting for?"

"I don't know if you were part of this, but I think we gave Ramona exactly what she wanted either way." I nudged Iris, her face suddenly redder than before.

"Stop talking about me when I can only hear one half of the argument," Iris said. "I did what I had to for Lou and for you."

I knew she did, but part of me wondered if there wasn't a small part of her that was curious about the demon who clearly had a soft spot in hell for her. Who wouldn't be curious about what a date with a demon would be like, right?

This whole thing was a mess and getting messier by the second.

We got up to the apartment and went our separate ways. Lou had taken to haunting the living room by night. She was keeping Ichabod company at least. I flung myself down on my bed to pull the blankets up to my chin and stare up to the ceiling. I let fantasies of Harlow and me together push the dread from my gut and put me to sleep.

21

HARLOW

It was midmorning and I had already had a big win for the day: I'd opened the café all by myself.

Willow had woken up with an uncharacteristic headache, and I had ordered her back to bed to get another hour's sleep before the morning rush. The fact that she'd even let me attempt to open the café was a big sign that she was beginning to trust me. . . or she was truly feeling awful.

A rap at the back door had me checking the old black and silver clock ticking beside the drinks menu.

"Right on time," I said, sashaying to the back door and opening the roller blind.

I must have forgotten to unlock the door when I opened. Wyatt offered me a lopsided grin and lifted the box of morning treats in his hand. I undid the three locks and flipped over the protection ward that the witches had gifted Willow when she'd moved to town. It had felt a little overkill when I'd first moved here, but now hearing about the alliance between the creatures of Maple Hollow, I was starting to think it was a good idea.

I held the door open for Wyatt, and he breezed in, his puppy-dog personality dampening a bit when he didn't see Willow.

"She's having a sleep-in," I said before he asked.

"Who?" Wyatt set the box on the counter. "You can't be talking about Willow."

"She's letting me open the shop," I said. "She has a headache."

Wyatt instinctively looked to the door that led up to her bedroom. I wondered if he'd ever been up there. He sniffed the air, his eyebrows pinching together in concern. "Yeah." He worried his bottom lip with his elongated canine. "She's sick."

"You can *smell* that she's sick?" The thought made me cringe. What else could he smell? I did a quick pit check, and Wyatt chuckled.

"I can't smell you—that much," he amended. "I'm tuned in to her scent."

"You're *tuned in to her scent*?" I balked, eyeing him up and down. "What the fuck does that mean?"

He gulped like he'd just spilled some big secret and quickly whirled to the box of treats. "Here are the cauldron macarons." He waved a hand down a row of treats.

"Very subtle deflection," I muttered, though my mouth watered just looking at them. "I want to eat all of them."

"At least let a few people try them before you eat the rest." Wyatt laughed. "Careful with transferring them into the cabinet. The assembly of broomstick to bristles is a little precarious."

I gave a nod. "Got it."

"And let me know how they go. If they're a hit, I'll make some more and maybe some other witchy treats."

The door to the upstairs opened, and Willow walked out

in her work uniform of jeans, T-shirt, and apron. She looked like she'd struggled to pull herself together—dark purple bags under her eyes, her gaze a little glassed over, her shoulders slumped, and her movements slow.

"You just couldn't help yourself," I said with a huff.

"Hey." Wyatt swept in and placed a tentative hand on her forearm, steadying her as if she might topple over. "Why don't you go back to bed? Harlow can manage today."

"No," Willow grumbled, rubbing the sleep from her eyes. "I'm fine. I just need a cup of coffee . . . or twelve." She paused at the countertop, her bloodshot eyes narrowing at the selection in the pastry box. "What are those?"

She pointed to the macaron cookies. Great. Even half-comatose, she still noticed the one tiny discrepancy in the order.

"I thought we could try something new for the food cabinet," I offered tentatively.

"You planned a new order? With Wyatt? Without me?"

I held up my hands in placation. "I just thought it would be fun to try something new."

"Fun?" Her voice rose. "Something new like when you added nutmeg to Agnes's coffee and almost killed her? That kind of fun?"

"I can take them away," Wyatt offered, but he went silent when Willow's gaze landed on him.

She turned her wrath back to me. "I had a carefully planned order. One that gives every patron an option while satisfying any allergies or dietary requirements. One that doesn't make the cabinet cluttered. One that sells." She placed a splayed hand on her chest. "I do what I do because it works. You changing things for *fun* has already lost me customers."

Heat rose in my cheeks, and tears pricked my eyes. The

pride I'd felt a moment ago turned into shame at my sister's anger.

"I'm sorry," I murmured. "I will do it exactly as you do. Really. You can go back to bed."

Willow scoffed. "I don't think so. I'm clearly needed down here." She barely glanced at Wyatt when she said, "You can go now."

"Willow." He reached for her, but she pulled away.

I made myself scarce, grabbing the broom and sweeping around the doorway, but I could hear Willow say, "You planned all this with my sister, without talking to me, even though you know how I don't like change? Even though you and I always talk through the menu together?"

"They're just cookies," Wyatt begged, and I thought he might drop to his knees at any second.

There was betrayal and hurt in my sister's eyes. "You of all people know how important this is to me." I swore I heard her voice wobble. "Tomorrow morning, leave the order at the back door."

"Willow." Wyatt said her name like he was pleading for mercy. "Please."

"Goodbye, Wyatt," she said and stormed off into the kitchen.

22

HARLOW

I swung my boots over the surface of the water, little bioluminescent lights seeming to track each movement. This place was like something out of a fairy tale. I wondered if a mermaid or a Jamaican crab would pop up from the water at any second.

Willow had warned me not to venture through the haunted forest, but I couldn't really see why. It was a little spooky at first, but I'd found a well-traveled trail that led to the docks and a massive lake that seemed to stretch in every direction.

I'd managed to hold it together for the rest of my shift, fighting back tears until after closing, but once all of my jobs had been finished, I'd thrown a noncommittal "I'm going out" over my shoulder and left.

Willow hadn't stopped me.

Things between Willow and me were frigid at best— worse than when I'd poisoned Agnes or accidentally conjured that plague of mice.

I couldn't believe she wouldn't even trust me with

fucking baked goods! *This* was the nail in the coffin of our relationship?

Was I really that much of a fuckup to her?

I'd debated leaving right then and there but couldn't convince my feet to make those final steps out the door. Even now, I was thinking about buying a bus ticket out of here. I wasn't meant to be in a town like this, or with a sibling who wouldn't let me take off the training wheels.

Though I was angry and hurt by what Willow had said, in the deepest parts of me, a voice whispered, *I probably deserve all of Willow's anger and disappointment. I don't deserve to be trusted. I'm not worthy of a relationship with her. I'm never going to be good enough.*

I was done. I just wanted to run away . . . again.

Then a louder realization hit, resonating over the dark gloom. "But then I'd miss that date at the pumpkin patch with Jordyn."

A shining silver thread was holding me here. After that kiss we'd shared, I would probably suffer another hundred days of disappointing Willow just to have another like that.

As if summoning her from my thoughts alone, I heard a creak on the boards and turned to see Jordyn walking toward me.

She paused when I spotted her, as if we were playing a silent game of red light, green light.

"I wasn't following you!" she said, shifting her weight awkwardly. "In case you were wondering."

"What are you doing out here?" I felt like a giant weight had been lifted off my chest at the sight of her.

I swore she was my own brand of magic, the way she could instantly ease my mind.

"I needed to get out of my apartment. Too . . . noisy. I needed to be alone with my thoughts for once."

"I know the feeling."

"I could go?" Jordyn asked, clearly misreading that statement. "If you want some peace?"

"No, stay! Please." I patted the splintering wooden slats beside me.

Her gaze landed on my hand but then traveled to the murky water below. "Let's go sit along the shore." She beckoned with her silver-ringed fingers. "Swamp monsters are the least of your concerns here. We wouldn't want one of the merfolk to pull you under into another dimension."

I quickly yanked my feet up, hugging my knees to my chest. "I didn't realize that was a possibility."

I frowned down at the water and then my eyes darted to a rickety fishing boat tied up at the end of the dock.

"It's safe to fish here?"

"Katie knows her way through the lake," Jordyn said. "She only fishes during the day and knows how to separate the magical creatures from the ... edible ones."

I shuddered at that. I was never looking at fish the same again. I warily stood and wandered toward Jordyn, taking in everything from her chunky knit cardigan to her black star-print tights to the hasty ponytail pulling back half her hair.

When I was a single step away, I said, "Hi."

Her red lips curved. "Hi."

With only a moment of hesitation, I leaned forward and brushed a soft kiss on her lips. She hummed against my mouth, and when I pulled back, she was smiling at me in a way that made my heart clench. When she looked at me like that, she made me feel like I was something special, something just as magical as she was.

Jordyn took my hand and led me off the dock and onto the grassy knoll clouded with dancing fireflies. "So what are you doing in the haunted forest—after dark, no less?"

"Willow and I had a fight," I said, and Jordyn's hand squeezed mine tighter in acknowledgment. "It was my fault. I should've asked for her permission before I did anything with her café. I thought I was being helpful. I just . . ." I scrubbed my free hand down my face. "Here," I said, taking off my jacket and throwing it down on the grass for us to sit on.

"Thanks," she said then got settled on the ground. "I'm sorry about what happened with Willow. That sounds really tough."

"I think it's mostly because I planned it with Wyatt behind her back."

"Ah." Jordyn nodded her head sagely as she leaned back on her elbows. "He should've known better."

I glanced at Jordyn. "What?"

"It's not really my place to say," she said with a sigh. "But, yeah, nothing about Wyatt and Willow is rational."

I chuckled. "I don't get why they don't just tell each other that they're into each other. It's so obvious."

Jordyn shuffled closer to my side. "Wyatt's father is the pack leader." My eyebrows shot up, and she let out the sweetest soft laugh that made my insides flutter. "Yeah, he isn't exactly what you'd think of when it comes to alpha males. But he's got a lot of future responsibilities on his shoulders. Ones he probably views as a burden and is trying to hide from. But it will all catch up with him sooner or later."

"I had no idea," I said softly. "I guess it's more complicated than I thought."

"There are some things in the werewolf community that he won't be able to run from, and it's understandable that he'd want to shield her from them, no matter what his heart is screaming."

Was she right? She would know better than I could, but shouldn't the leader of the pack be entitled to the right to choose who he fell in love with?

"I suspect that's part of your sister's response," Jordyn mused.

"Ugh. I just can't stop messing things up—even more than I normally do." I stared out at the glowing water. The moon peeked through the thick swathes of trees above us. "There are so many unwritten rules in a place like this. I don't think I'll last in this town long," I added bitterly.

"Oh." Jordyn sounded legitimately disappointed, and I wished I could take back what I'd said.

I felt like a dick. None of this was her fault. "I mean, this is a town of the paranormal. I don't fit in here."

Jordyn took my hand again, and my muscles eased at the warmth of her touch. "You fit," she said quietly, eyeing me up and down. She looked back at the lake and added so quietly that I wasn't sure if my mind was playing tricks on me, "You fit with me." She cleared her throat. "Besides, we need more people like you around here."

"People like what?"

"Fun, energetic, beautiful, brave . . ."

Despite the shadowed forest, I knew from the way her nose wrinkled that she was blushing.

"I'm not brave," I said with a shake of my head.

Jordyn tugged me back to lie across my jacket, and she folded into my side, resting her head on my shoulder. It felt better than stepping into a hot bath after a long day. She fit into my side like the missing piece to a puzzle.

"I don't know many people who would be willing to investigate a paranormal murder, volunteer to go meet a demon, or chitchat with a monster like Billy over coffee."

Jordyn's words vibrated into my chest. "You might be the bravest person I know."

I huffed.

"I'm serious," she said, playfully swatting at me. "You make me feel . . ." She let out a long, slow sigh. "You make me feel steady, like everything's going to be okay. Does that make sense? Goddess, I'm rambling. I'm probably not explaining—"

I leaned down and kissed her again, silencing her doubts. Then I let the kiss linger a little longer. "You make sense to me," I murmured against her lips.

When I pulled away an inch, she was giving me that look again. The one that made me feel like she saw right to the very center of my soul. She looked at me like she saw me in a way that no one else ever had.

God, I wanted to touch every inch of her skin and make her unravel under my touch. Another night, I would have. But right now, it was so sweet and slow and sacred, so I would save the passion. Tonight, I'd just relish the rise and fall of her steady breaths and the sound of crickets chirping and the frogs singing in the darkness of the nighttime forest.

I tucked her closer into my side. She was so utterly perfect, I wondered if she'd been molded from moondust to be my dream girl. She saw *me*. And I saw her.

I decided then and there that there would be no bus tickets.

I knew I'd be in trouble if I fell asleep and didn't make it to my shift in time tomorrow morning, which might be the least of my problems if some monsters were prowling the forest tonight . . . but with Jordyn in my arms, I felt safe. I drifted asleep under the stars while holding her to my chest, feeling all of a sudden like here, in a literal haunted forest, was the most I'd ever felt at home.

23
JORDYN

I waited on a hay bale, my legs swinging along to the tune that Lou was humming from where she stood next to it. I tried to ignore her like an unwelcome radio. I was still buzzing after spending the night with Harlow in the forest. Which had ended unceremoniously when the sun had peeked between the trees and Harlow had looked at her watch, given me one last quick kiss, and bolted off to the café.

I'd spent the rest of the day as a bundle of nerves. If Lou had known I'd snuck out of the apartment last night, she hadn't let on, and if she'd figured it out, she would've teased me relentlessly for it. She'd tease me even more if she knew all the sappy thoughts floating around in my head.

The way Harlow made me feel . . . I was already in deep trouble. It was like I'd spent my whole life staring at the moon and she'd walked in with all of her sunshine. Now I was constantly seeking out her warmth, constantly turning toward the sun.

Even now, in the late afternoon with a few short hours

of day left, I was waiting on top of an itchy cube of hay just to spend a few shiny moments with her.

The local pumpkin patch was always full of the largest and most perfectly rotund pumpkins. A coven elder cast a spell on the patch to make it abundant year-round. Even in the height of summer, tourists could come pumpkin picking.

Around front were freshly picked pumpkins for those who didn't want to forage for their own in the field. Throughout the patch stood stacked hay bales and scare-crows—perfect spots for snapping a photo for social media along with signs clearly displaying Maple Hollow's social media handles. A giant apple-shaped kiosk sold spiced cider and candied apples from the haunted orchard. Beside it sat a long table of serrated knives, cookie cutters, and paint for making the perfect jack-o'-lantern.

At the entry gate was Juniper. She didn't exactly look like the outgoing, customer service-savvy pumpkin patch entrepreneur she was. With pallid gray skin, spider webbing circles around her eyes, and slimy green seaweed woven through her hair, Juniper looked like every other swamp monster, but she was peppier than a hopped-up Easter Bunny, and the tourists loved her, no matter that she smelled like a bog. Juniper had been more than a little surprised when I'd shown up here.

I looked all around me and started wondering if this was corny. Locals didn't usually go on dates here. This was more of a tourist hotspot . . . but Harlow was new in town, and everyone should go pumpkin picking at least once in their lifetime. Plus, we were upholding the ruse of finding the perfect window-sized ones for Witch's Brew Café. Maybe we could find some squashes and gourds too and go for a walk along the dark forest to collect some leaves to decorate the windowsills. I bet she'd love that.

By the moon, Harlow was already ten minutes late. A knot of nerves formed in my stomach. "When she arrives, you're leaving, right?"

"That's what we agreed." Lou walked straight through the hay bale and toed a pumpkin with her loafer. "Do you think she got spooked by Ramona? Do you think she's going to stand you up?"

"Why would you ask me that?"

"Because you seem nervous. It's cute."

"Maybe I'm nervous because you're lurking."

"I'm a ghost. We lurk." Lou snorted. "Speak of the devil."

I looked up to see Harlow walking through the front gate. Her short hair was covered by a rust-red beanie, which complemented her red flannel button-down. She wore her usual ripped jeans and combat boots and looked ridiculously adorable with her shoulders bunched up around her ears and whorls of steam circling her head.

"Sorry. Sorry." This seemed to be her trademark greeting. "I had to give some tourists directions," she explained after she'd crossed the distance to me. "The B&B *is* that way, right?" She pointed in the opposite direction of the B&B, and Lou snickered.

"Yep," I said because I didn't want to crush her spirits. I rose from the squat hay bale and bridged the last stretch between us. "Hi."

Her rosy cheeks lifted. "Hi."

We leaned in simultaneously, and I brushed a light kiss across her lips. It was so soft and gentle, making my whole body tingle. I wanted to pull her into the darkest corner of the pumpkin patch and melt into her touch, but I held myself together.

I glanced behind me and realized Lou was still there, watching me with a smug expression.

"So, pumpkins," I offered. "Uh, the midsized ones are over there. Why don't you get started and I'll go grab us some shears in case we want to cut our own?"

"Oh, okay." She narrowed her eyes at me for a second as I offered her a sheepish smile, but she gratefully wandered off.

"You seriously need to give me some space, Lou," I growled under my breath as I marched to the table. "I'm going to scare her away if I keep acting like this. You—" I turned around and realized Lou was gone. Of *course* she chose to disappear on me mid-tirade. "Asshole." I realized I was too close to a family who were carving pumpkins and I grimaced. "Sorry."

Juniper patted one of the kids on the shoulder and said, "I'll be right back." Then she wandered over to me with a wide smile. "Well, look what the crows brought in." She gave me a once-over. "You're a bit dressed up for the scarecrows, aren't you?"

I looked down at my outfit. I'd put more effort into my appearance than normal, but was it too much for an outdoor date?

"Thanks," I answered. "I guess."

"You got my gift basket?"

I offered her a smile. "Yes, thank you."

Juniper was well-meaning if not somewhat misguided in her attempts to maintain our friendship with gift baskets. We were already friends; I didn't need gifts. But ever since Lou had died, Juniper had insisted on bringing me gifts and looking out for me more than anyone else in town.

"So what brings you here? I don't think you've come

down to this pumpkin patch of your own volition since our second-grade field trip," she said with a chuckle.

The wind shifted direction, and I got a big whiff of Juniper's signature perfume. She had it made specifically to enhance the green aroma and mask the algae that collected in her stringy hair. But there was some other note underneath that I couldn't quite place.

"Harlow's never been here before," I said, tipping my head toward the red beanie in the distance.

"Harlow?"

"I guess you haven't met her yet." I drummed my fingers across the table nervously. "She's Willow Miller's sister."

Juniper inclined her head. "A human?"

"Yeah," I murmured, remembering the alliance Ramona spoke of. It sounded like the monsters supported the idea of getting rid of the human residents of Maple Hollow. "That's not a problem, is it?"

Juniper's eerie green eyes focused on me, her smile faltering. "Why would that be a problem?"

My stomach soured at that smile, and I wondered if she knew we'd fallen asleep by the lake. If anyone would, it would be her. And then she'd tell the whole town about how I fell asleep with a human in the forest. "Oh, I don't know." I quickly grabbed the sharpest gardening shears I could find. "I should go catch up to Harlow before she canvases the whole patch. See ya, Juniper." I turned before the swamp monster could say anything more and raced toward Harlow.

"Got them," I said, waving the shears in proof.

"So is there an art to pumpkin picking?" Harlow asked with that gorgeous, little grin that made her cheeks dimple. "Do I have to knock on them like melons or . . ."

I *really* wanted to say that I'd love to knock on her melons, but after the shears debacle, I decided against it.

"Check the skin," I said. "Nothing too wrinkly or over-ripe." I pointed to one that looked like melted candle wax. "Definitely nothing like that. Better to go a bit greener and let it ripen on the sill."

Harlow winked at me. Goddess, I loved it when she winked. "A pumpkin connoisseur."

"It's as compulsory as learning your ABCs here." I shrugged. "It comes with the whole witchy thing."

She laughed. "I should get your advice on broomsticks and candles too."

"Careful." I pointed at her. "Don't get me started or I'll never stop."

Her smile broadened. "I think I'd like to see that."

Ugh. My witchy bits were fluttering. How did she do that? Be so freaking charming without even trying?

"So, I'm thinking four medium pumpkins for the windows and a bunch of little ones for the tables." She bent and picked up two pumpkins and held them up like fake boobs. "Hmm . . ." I guffawed as she weighed them up and down. "No, not right." She set them back down.

I watched as she examined a few others. "You're taking this very seriously."

"Willow is trusting me with the decorations," she said, digging through a barrel of miniature, speckled yellow gourds. "Begrudgingly," she added.

"Wow." I rocked back on my heels. "I'm surprised Willow would relinquish any control over the café. She's an overprotective mother hen for that place."

"I think this is her way of trying. Although after today, I don't know how much more trusting she'll be doing," Harlow replied. "Ooh!" She held up a bedazzled pumpkin that looked like a disco ball.

"Are you trying to give Willow an aneurysm?"

"Good point." She set the pumpkin back on the display table. "Okay, maybe more traditional." She grabbed a wicker basket filled with an assortment of mini-pumpkins and looked at me for approval.

"I think they're perfect," I said with a nod. "Now for the medium ones?"

"I think we should venture farther into the patch." She hooked her thumb at the shadowed field behind her. "The pre-picked ones all look a bit ready to turn."

"A discerning eye. We'll make a pumpkin connoisseur out of you yet." I chuckled and followed her.

We wandered through the fields until we were past the braziers that heated customers as they stomped through the field. Harlow swung her basket as she walked, veering toward a stack of hay bales that formed the far wall of the patch. Harlow stepped over a bale, sat down, and set her basket beside her.

"There's no pumpkins out there," I said.

"I know." Her shoulders tensed. "But it's quiet." She glanced at me and patted the spot beside her.

It was such an endearing movement that I climbed over and sat beside her without hesitation. Straw poked at the backs of my legs, and I really wished I'd worn something thicker than my black leggings.

I stared up at the moon. It grew brighter with every breath as my eyes adjusted to the darkness around us. It suddenly became abundantly clear why Harlow brought me out here: to be alone.

I reached over and grabbed her hand, her fingers instantly intertwining with mine.

She hummed, squeezing my hand. "I like this . . . I like you."

Goddess, I felt like I was in middle school again. "I like you too. A lot."

There was something so gentle and sweet about her, something slower than the instant fire I'd had with Lou. I liked just holding Harlow's hand and staring up at the same night sky that I'd watched my entire life. She brought something new to the mundane. I could've sat there all night if that was what she wanted, but my stomach flipped anew with butterflies as she leaned closer and kissed me.

Her mouth fused with mine, and her tongue brushed the seam of my lips, making me open for her. Her tongue plundered my mouth as mine eagerly licked back, the fingers of my free hand curling in her shirt and tugging her closer. Her hand dropped to my hip, and she practically hoisted me toward her.

I was so fucking grateful that she'd made the first move. Or had I by kissing her when she'd arrived? No, that'd been a chaste kiss. *This* was an all-consuming, "I'm-ready-to-fuck" kind of kiss and it was turning my blood molten with desire.

She tugged me toward her until I was hinging forward. I climbed into her lap, straddling her with one knee between her legs. I didn't give a single fuck about the straw that bit into my knee as I kissed her and ground against her leg. I was already so wet for her. This was ridiculous. Was she seriously non-magical? Because this was a spell if ever there was one.

She rocked her hips in rhythm with mine, rolling against my knee. Sweet pumpkin pie, I loved the friction against the ripped denim of her thigh. Harlow's hand snaked up my short velvet dress, skimming up to my bra.

She broke our kiss for the briefest moment to murmur, "Is this okay?" against my mouth as she cupped my breast.

I hummed against her lips. "Yes. Touch me." I rocked

faster as her hand dipped into the cup of my bra and her fingers circled my nipple, pulling a moan from my lips.

My fingers squeezed the back of her neck in response as she twirled my peaked nipple with her fingers.

Fuck.

I was so close, and I could feel how feverish she was for more. Taking it slow wasn't going to be as easy as I'd hoped. I needed to feel her hands and mouth and skin. I pulled at her shirt, but it wasn't enough. I wanted far fewer layers between us. I broke our kiss to scan the pumpkin patch to see if there was any place that wasn't covered in spiny pumpkin vines or spiky hay, but as my gaze lifted back toward the bright lights of the main area of the patch, I found a lone figure standing in the middle of the field.

The heat of my blood cooled instantly and a pain hit my chest.

Lou watched us with her arms folded tightly across her chest, tears in her eyes. A mixture of anger and something else was etched on her face. Confusion, maybe? Sorrow? Betrayal? She'd been pushing me into this, yet she looked like I'd just broken her heart all over again. Could you hurt a ghost?

I leaped up, straightening my shirt.

"What?" Harlow asked, searching the fields around us, but of course, she didn't see anything.

"Nothing, I . . ." I balled my hands into fists. "I'm sorry. I've got to go."

I raced off, leaving yet another woman with confusion and sorrow in her eyes.

24
JORDYN

"You broke our agreement!" I screamed at Lou from the safety of my apartment. "What the hell was that? You made me act like a dick to Harlow! Just staring at me like that, what the fuck? I thought you wanted me to move on!"

Lou huffed out a breath and scrubbed a hand down her face in a gesture I knew meant she was trying not to lose her temper. "I don't know what I'm doing here anymore."

"What?" I barked. "What does that even mean?"

Harlow's disappointed face flashed through my mind again, and it made my anger surge higher. How was I going to explain this away? Would she let me try to make it up to her?

Lou gestured around the room. "I don't think I can handle watching you fall in love with someone else."

"You've *thrown* the two of us together and now you're out?" Didn't Lou say that was why she was stuck?

She just leaned against my dresser and crossed her arms.

"Then why can't you leave, Lou?" My mind was racing

and grasping for any sort of sense but came up empty. "If you're angry that I'm moving on, then that should mean you can go back to the afterlife, right?"

"You summoned me here to torture me, didn't you?" Her voice was calm at first, then turned to venom. "Is this your last nail in my coffin, Jordyn? You've trapped me in this twisted little world of yours and now I have to stay here and watch you fuck someone else!"

With a deafening crack, the dresser behind her erupted into splinters. Clothes and trinkets scattered to the corners of my bedroom.

I jolted backward, my eyes flaring. "What the fuck, Lou?"

Something like fear passed over Lou's face when she realized what she'd done. Frantic footsteps from somewhere in the apartment came rushing toward us.

"Goddess, Jordyn!" Iris called behind the closed door. "Are you okay?" She let herself in and shrieked. "Holy shit!"

"Lou did it," I told Iris. "You owe me a new dresser, bitch. I don't know how, but you better find some cash in your ghostly pockets or start commanding power tools."

"That's not what I screamed at." Iris pointed directly at Lou, her eyes wide. "I can see her."

"What?" Lou and I exclaimed in unison.

Iris's gaze panned up and down Lou's more solid form. Both of them seemed pleasantly surprised by the new manifestation of Lou's corporal being. To me, it was like I'd adjusted a camera's focus so she was more vivid than before. The color of her hair was less dull, her skin refreshed and less grey.

"Oh man, Lou." Iris finally found her voice. "What an outfit to die in. You look hot as ever. Wait, is that Jordyn's shirt?"

"You better be kidding," I yelled at Iris. "Are you hitting on a ghost? My ghost ex?"

Iris peeked at me. "It doesn't hurt to be polite."

Seriously? First Ramona, and now Lou? Iris would hit on anything—with or without a pulse.

"This can't be possible," I said. "She shouldn't be visible to anyone who wasn't present at the summoning. And how has she managed to explode my dresser?"

I wasn't sure who I was asking, but I looked at Iris to confirm I wasn't actually going crazy and that Lou hadn't broken any universal laws of nature.

Iris chewed her lip for a second before her eyebrows shot up. "Did you make her angry?"

"Uh, kind of," I said. "She caught me and Harlow hooking up in the pumpkin patch."

"Oh my goddess," Iris squealed. "You have to give me all the details." She glanced at Lou. "Later."

Lou bared her clenched teeth, and the room started shaking like a train was whizzing by just beside the wall. Ichabod hissed from somewhere in the living room followed by a terrified growl. The love he had for his invisible playmate was gone now.

Lou made a creaking gurgling that made my stomach plunge with ice.

"Iris," I muttered from the corner of my mouth, "what is happening to her?"

"I-I think . . . she's turning into a vengeful spirit."

"We can't let that happen." I grabbed for Iris's arm and pulled her to my side. "We have to stop her."

"We need to help her cross over—and fast."

Together, we took several steps toward the living room where we kept our most powerful magical ingredients. But the moment my foot hit the threshold, Lou's image flickered in and out like static on an old TV. Then the rumbling stopped. The color drained from her appearance and she looked all around. "What just happened?" Lou asked.

"I can't see her anymore," Iris whispered.

Relief hit me but left behind a stone in my gut. "You just had a little bit of a meltdown. Don't you remember?"

"No." Lou looked behind her and pointed at the splinters and scattered clothes all around her feet. "Who did that?"

"You did." I narrowed my eyes at her. "Because of what happened at the pumpkin patch."

"Why would the pumpkin patch make me blow up your dresser?"

"You were mad about Harlow and me, uh, kissing." I honestly didn't want to remind Lou about the teenage-level grinding Harlow and I had done in the middle of an open field.

And then I'd run off like a coward.

I needed to find Harlow and explain myself. Just not with the truth. *Fuck!*

"You said you didn't think you were actually here for me to move on with Harlow?" I asked gently, trying to jog Lou's memory. Did ghosts have memories?

"I told you it was about her death!" Iris insisted. "Ghosts don't hang around to see their exes shack up with someone else. Sometimes it's to say goodbye to a loved one, but usually it's because they want vengeance for a violent end. And we know someone murdered her. That's why she's still here."

"We need to solve this murder, then—and quick," I said. "Before she hulks out again."

"Well, we know it's a local," Iris said. "We've got our list of suspects from the square and Ramona's info about this antihuman alliance..."

I turned to Lou. "But you don't remember anything that happened that day?" I prompted. "Try and think. You said something about brunch."

Lou squeezed her eyes shut. "It's like a dream that I can't quite remember, only a feeling." She took a deep, silent breath, no real air filling her lungs. "We were eating at a café. I had the big veggie breakfast . . . halloumi, roasted tomatoes, poached eggs—" She opened her eyes. "And someone had a bagel with lox."

"Who's we?" I asked.

"Huh?"

"You said 'we were eating at a café,'" I replied. "Do you remember who was sitting across from you?"

She closed her eyes again. "I remember the smell of fresh paint. Splatters across leather boots. Maple syrup . . . but that could've just been from the breakfast. Maybe they had pancakes?"

"Then who had the bagel?" Iris asked. "Was there more than one of them?"

Lou stomped her foot, and it collided against the floorboards instead of going through like it normally would have.

I groaned. "Please don't kick a hole in my floor."

"Your ability to physically manipulate the space is growing with your anger," Iris said. "Try to control it."

"I'm trying," Lou gritted out.

"Is it possible . . ." I held up my hand to Lou. "Could you just go float downstairs for a second?"

She glowered at me, but her body floated downward until she disappeared.

I turned to Iris. "Do spirits normally not remember the

day they died? Is it possible someone used magic to make her forget? She didn't have anything in her system when she died. At least nothing that they test for."

Iris frowned at me. "I don't talk to that many spirits, Jordyn. I don't normally canvas the ghosts that I *do* summon either."

I blew out a frustrated sigh. "Well, I guess we've got to summon another one to ask."

"You're kidding, right?" Iris cocked her hip. "You want to risk summoning another spirit that may or may not hang around for who knows how long? Why don't you ask the rest of the coven for help?"

I frantically waved at the spot where Lou had just disappeared. "Because then I'll have to explain how I royally screwed up. The last thing I need is a lecture from my mother on top of all of this."

Iris glowered at me for a moment before she threw her hands up in the air. "Fine. But I'm doing the summoning circle this time! You've proven you can't be trusted to do it on your own for a while."

I stared at the splintered dresser, reliving the look on both Lou's and Harlow's faces. I should have already informed our coven elders about what I'd done, but the disappointment and embarrassment would be too much for me to bear. Iris and I were supposed to be training to take over high-ranking positions in our circle, but instead we were hiding a ghost I'd summoned for selfish reasons.

Iris snapped her fingers in front of me. "Hey. Focus."

"Sorry, I just . . ." The stone in my gut made it too difficult for me to describe what I was feeling.

Which must have been written on my face because instead of scolding me, Iris said, "Why don't you go talk to

Harlow. I'll do the summoning. Your energy is off, and we don't need bad intentions in the air. It could mess up my spell work."

She grabbed me by the shoulders and steered me out the door.

"I'll keep Lou company," I said. "You take your time."

25
HARLOW

The bristles of my scrub brush raked over the wooden tabletop over and over again. Not that there was a crumb left, but my frustration cleaning was going to make every surface shine.

I'd walked around the square for an hour before I'd decided I needed to drown out the noise of countless questions with soap, water, and the shop radio. The local station played Halloween music year-round, but as I'd come to discover after two hours of cleaning, there really weren't that many Halloween classics. "Monster Mash" was starting up for the fourth time when I heard the radio click off. I popped my head up to see Willow leaning against the doorframe, her golden-blonde hair a frazzled mess as she arched a quizzical brow at me.

"What'd that table ever do to you?" She tugged on the belt of her bathrobe, squeezing the blob of blue terrycloth into an hourglass figure.

I stared down at my rubber gloves white-knuckling a

scrubber, the bucket of cleaning solution still rippling from my vigorous dunking.

"I'm just doing a deep clean," I said tightly.

She looked at the gleaming floors, countertops, and espresso machine. "Something must be really wrong if you're cleaning at two a.m." Willow wandered over to the cupboard and grabbed two teacups. "Talk to me."

"I don't want tea," I muttered, but my sister went about her ritual of filling two cups with chamomile and milk regardless. When she finished, she walked to the other side of the booth from where I was sitting. She set the teacups down with practiced ease, barely a clink of the ceramic on the table.

Willow picked up her cup and blew on the hot drink as she looked at me through curls of steam. "This doesn't have anything to do with a certain brunette witch who works at an apothecary, does it?"

"Maybe," I hedged as I peeled off the soaking-wet sweatshirt that was clinging to my body for dear life.

She took another sip and watched me over the rim of her cup. "I'm guessing pumpkin picking didn't go that well?"

I gestured to the half-empty basket next to the register. "It went great until it didn't."

She gave the small gourds an approving nod before turning back to me. "What happened?"

"That's the thing," I grumbled. "I have no idea. We were making out on a hay bale"—my sister chuckled into her tea —"and next thing I know, she jumps off me like she's seen a ghost and says she has to go."

"I mean, how hot and heavy was it? Maybe it was too far too fast?"

I wiped at a little scuff on the table. "It seemed like she

was into it. I . . . I'd feel like an asshole if I misread the whole thing."

"Jordyn is a complicated one," Willow said. "There's a reason she hasn't dated in over a year."

I raised a brow at her. "What's that supposed to mean?"

My sister was protective, but I got the feeling she hadn't had more than a few short conversations with Jordyn in the years she'd lived here. They both worked long hours as local business managers. How many friends could you make with their schedules?

Willow looked as if she were considering her words carefully. "Jordyn has always struggled with trusting anyone outside the coven."

It was a diplomatic answer. A nonanswer answer.

"Why?"

A flash of surprise covered her face as she looked past me. "Looks like you get to ask her that yourself."

I looked out the window to see Jordyn pacing the sidewalk. I battled with the urge to run to my room and hide— or fling the open door and demand answers.

Willow got to her feet and gave Jordyn a small wave before turning to the stairs at the back of the café. "I'm just going to go back to bed," she said with the smallest amount of subtlety possible. "Go talk to her." And then she shut the door loud enough for the whole neighborhood to hear.

At the sound, Jordyn's eyes locked with mine.

Thanks, Willow. Really nice.

I awkwardly walked to the door to open it, but Jordyn paused at the threshold.

"Are you debating bolting again?" I internally scolded myself at how harsh the words came out.

"That seems to be what I do best these days," she answered before taking a definitive step inside.

I rolled my eyes. "What happened tonight, Jordyn? Why did you wig out?"

She blew out a long breath and leaned against the wall. "Cutting straight to the chase, I guess?"

"Oh, I'm sorry. Did you come here to talk about the local choir practice? Best brand of tampon?" I folded my arms. "I don't want to play games. Why are you here?"

"Okay, so I'm guessing you get more sarcastic when you're angry?"

"What insight!" I crowed, even though I knew I was just confirming what she suggested. "Where's your crystal ball?"

"I didn't think you'd be this mad—"

"I'm not mad!" I barked in a tone that did, indeed, sound mad. "I'm just confused and upset. Can't you see it from my side? Every time we get a moment of alone time and it feels like things are heating up, you get all freaked out. It feels weird and gross when you're mid-make out and the person you're kissing just bolts without any explanation." I held my side and sucked in a deep breath after that long rant.

Jordyn's brows pinched together like what I'd said was paining her. "I'm sorry . . . I want to talk about it. But . . ." She shuffled her feet and wrapped her arms around herself.

"Did I do something wrong?"

Her eyes snapped to mine, surprise replacing the unease. "You did nothing wrong."

In two steps, she had my cheeks in her hands and was pulling me into a fierce kiss.

I wrapped my arms around her, feeling the soft curves of her breasts against mine and the squirm of her hips in my hold. She pulled back, and I searched for reluctance but only saw blazing lust.

"Don't stop," I said breathlessly, pulling her into me again. It probably wasn't the smartest way to resolve a conflict, but after all that pent-up anxiety, it felt good to have her lips on mine again.

I tugged her behind the counter, pinning her against it as I kissed her ravenously. She tasted like cinnamon and chocolate, the perfect blend of spice and decadence. The musk of our sweat mingled to make the perfect blend of sex and sweetness. If I could, I would have worn the scent of us as perfume for the rest of my life.

Desperation to feel her bare skin on mine was sinking in. I shoved off her jacket as her hands dropped to my belt, both of us thinking the same thing at the exact same time.

"Wait," I murmured against her fervent mouth. "Come with me." I pulled her by the wrist, leading her through the kitchen and toward my room.

Jordyn barely took a second to take in the space before her lips were back on mine. "Is your sister going to hear us?" she asked between kisses.

"Listen," I said, leaning my forehead against hers. Over the roaring of my heart, I could hear the chainsaw snores of my sister echoing from above. "She could sleep through a heavy metal concert playing in the corner."

"Thank the fucking Goddess." Jordyn pulled at my clothes and pressed her warm lips to my neck. "I've wanted you so badly from the moment I saw you stumble into the apothecary." She trailed up to my jaw as she hooked her fingers into my pants and shoved them down. "I'm sorry I freaked out earlier—"

"Apologize later, I need you now."

"Or in between rounds," she suggested as she tugged on the hem of my shirt.

I felt like the cat who got the cream with her promise of multiple orgasms. I yanked my shirt over my head as she did the same, undressing each other until we were bare. The bed creaked under our weight then settled when Jordyn lay on her back under me.

She was fucking gorgeous. Her long brown hair fanned out over the pillow, those rich hazel eyes locked on mine. Her gloriously soft skin, full breasts, and perfectly peaked nipples made my mouth water. She radiated erotic beauty that had heat pooling in my core. I swore she'd hypnotized me, and the way her eyes hooded as she looked up at me told me that she was thinking the exact same thing.

I dropped my mouth to kiss her collarbone, then trailed down to her breast. "I'm going to explore every inch of this stunning body," I vowed as I sucked one nipple into my mouth.

She arched against me, the fingers of one hand threading through my hair as the other trailed down my back. I released one nipple to lavish the other, my clit throbbing with anticipation as I worked her into a frenzy.

I moved lower, kissing a trail down her belly. Jordyn's breathing hitched the closer I grew to her core, her body trembling under me.

"I'm going to make you feel so good, little witch," I murmured against her skin. I nipped at her hip, moving my mouth tauntingly closer to her core and then straying away again.

"Please," Jordyn whispered, bucking her hips and squirming as if trying to direct my mouth to her dripping pussy.

"Please what?" I blew across her waxed flesh, her skin rippling with goose bumps.

She groaned. "Fuck me, Harlow."

"Ask and you shall receive," I taunted, brushing a kiss to her mound.

I wanted to hear her say it. I wanted no confusion this

time. I wanted it to be perfectly clear that I was doing exactly what she wanted me to do. Even if her body was telling me all the right things, nothing got me off more than hearing a hot girl demanding pleasure from me.

"Don't stop," she panted, and that wanton demand unleashed me.

I dropped to my forearms, spreading her wider, opening her like my own fucking feast. I gave one long, lingering lick up her sex that made her cry out before focusing my attention on her swollen clit.

"Goddess!" Jordyn shouted, her hand fisting into my hair as my tongue worked her over.

I circled her in slow licks, building speed with the increasingly desperate sounds she made, rewarding her for each moan. I sucked her clit and she mewled, gripping my hair tighter.

She was the sweetest fucking violin, and God, I loved playing her.

"More," she pleaded. "I need more."

I hummed my pleasure against her, wanting her to know exactly how much I loved it when she told me what she wanted. I circled two fingers around her sopping entrance, then dipped in and out, working my way deeper and massaging her inner walls. The sound of her moans set me on fire.

With my other hand, I slid my fingers over my clit, desperate for some relief from the building pressure.

Fuck, I might come just from her sounds alone. Who knew fucking a witch could be so good? This was truly otherworldly.

I kept my rhythm steady until she was teetering on the edge. Her muscles were already flickering over my fingers, and I knew she was close to release. I added a little more pressure with my tongue, circling her clit in a way that pulled those long, low moans from her. I hooked my fingers inside her a little more, and that was all it took.

She shattered, coming undone, her pussy clenching around my fingers.

I rubbed myself faster, my own orgasm ripping through me, the rush of pressure giving way to euphoria.

Jordyn's head dropped back onto the pillow, and she slung her forearm over her eyes. "Holy Goddess, Harlow," she panted. "That was incredible."

I kissed my way up her belly and rested there, letting the tension of my body ease against the smooth skin of her stomach. I loved hearing the rush of her heartbeat under my ear as my head rose and fell with each of her deep breaths.

And in that moment, a little knot formed in my stomach because I knew this was going to be more than sex between us. This witch was going to capture my heart.

I rubbed my eyes, enjoying the calm before our next round. My hands idly trailed down Jordyn's smooth sides, tracing the dips in her hips and the swells of her thighs. But when I opened my eyes, I jolted into a seated position.

There was someone standing in the corner of the room, watching us. The vision flickered, and I screamed.

Jordyn bolted upright. "What is it?"

I pointed to the apparition in the corner. "Ghost!"

26

JORDYN

A scream rang in my ears, and I realized it was my own, my throat shredding as Harlow's body flew across the room.

"Lou!" I shouted as Lou pinned Harlow to the wall. "Put her down! Now!"

Harlow's feet kicked out fruitlessly, only connecting with air and a small dresser.

"Lou?" Harlow croaked, her hands flying to her neck and clawing. "As in your dead ex-girlfriend, Lou?"

"It's a long story." I panted out the words. "Just let me save your ass, then I'll explain."

"Why don't you just tell her now, Jords?" Lou's voice echoed and rasped as if she were speaking through a fire.

"Jords is a terrible nickname," Harlow croaked. Then she was pulled off the wall and shoved back against it by any invisible force. "Jokes later, got it."

"Tell her!" Lou wailed, her eyes flaring to white. "Tell her why you're with her."

Fuck.

"I will tell her right now, okay, Lou?" I held up beseeching hands to her. "Just put her down."

Harlow's body slid up the wall like something straight out of a horror movie.

"Put her down before I break her, you mean?" Lou said in a sickening singsong.

"Yes. Please," I begged.

Lou's eyes snapped to mine. Her dark pupils ate up her irises until they were thin slivers of wispy brown. Her hands released Harlow, who screamed as she fell from the ceiling and onto the bed. Bouncing wildly, she flailed to the edge and wrapped a sheet around herself.

"And I thought my exes were fucked up!" she growled as she hastily stood and dressed.

"I've let her go, Jords," Lou said. "Now tell her why I'm here. Better yet, tell her why *you're* here. With her."

My head reared back like I'd been struck. *Fuck.* She was going to make me tell Harlow.

"Why you're here?" Harlow rubbed a hand across her throat. "What does that mean?"

I whirled toward her and then realized I was still butt-ass naked. I grabbed my jacket and put it on.

"I summoned Lou to say goodbye," I said carefully, folding my arms to keep the jacket closed. Both of these women had seen me nude, but I didn't want my tits hanging out while I explained what was happening. "But after I said goodbye, she wouldn't leave."

"Why not?" Harlow darted looks between Lou and me.

"She was trapped here and couldn't move on because she had unresolved business," I said. "We thought it was one thing, but then we realized she was murdered, and now we think she can't move on until her killer is brought to justice." I looked at Lou. "And with every passing day, she's getting more and more vengeful. I worry she won't be able to control it soon." The room trembled as Lou's anger flared again. "See what I mean?"

I gestured to the windowpane that trembled in its frame. Lou blinked and the shaking stopped. She folded her arms over her chest and hung her head. "I can't control it much longer, Jords. I'm afraid of what all this anger is going to do to me."

"Go back to the apothecary, Lou," I said firmly. "Go find Iris. I'll be back soon. Just let me talk to Harlow, okay?"

Lou swallowed and nodded. "Okay." She glanced at Harlow and waved up to the ceiling. "Sorry about the exorcist stuff." She turned and walked through the wall.

"This might be the worst ending to a hookup I've ever had," Harlow muttered as she picked up my clothes and threw them at me.

"Might be?" I asked incredulously. "There might be something else that comes close?"

"Another time," she said, sounding a little defeated. "In the pumpkin patch . . . I told Willow it looked like you'd seen a ghost. I guess you really had."

"Yeah," I said tightly.

"So she's what you've been glaring and muttering at all this time?"

"You noticed that, huh?"

"It must suck having your ex-girlfriend hovering around you while you date someone else."

I jumped my pants up over my thighs and grabbed my shoes. "Yep."

"What did she mean about you being here?"

I glanced up. Harlow was waiting for a reply, though she looked like she already knew. It felt like a sucker punch to the gut.

"I broke up with Lou because I was afraid to commit and then she died and I never got to move on and . . ." I sighed and swept my hair off my face. "And she thought that meant she had to help me move on with someone else. The first person to walk into the apothecary was you. She knocked that bottle off the shelf the other day. She wanted to set us up so that she could move on."

Harlow's eyes misted, and it made my heart crack open. "So you were only dating me to get rid of the ghost of your ex? God, that feels weird to say out loud." Harlow threw her hands up in the air as a tear streamed down her cheek. "This fucking town! You were just tricking me the whole time?"

"No, Harlow." I took a step forward and reached for her. "Baby. Please don't cry."

She sobbed at that. "Don't fucking 'baby' me." She shoved me away. "Just go. I can deal with a ghost, but I can't deal with the girl I'm fucking lying to me about it."

"You can deal with a ghost?"

She glared at me. "Everyone in this town acts like I can't handle this. Willow acts like I can't handle working at the café. The townspeople give me a wide berth like I can't handle their secrets because I'm a human and that makes me less than. I mean, yeah, Billy was a bit of a shock at first, I'll admit, and that swamp monster, Juniper, but everyone treats me like I'm a fucking damsel in distress, as if I'm always so unreliable—"

"I know you're not," I said, unsure if I should take a step toward or away from her.

Goddess, the woman had given me one of the best orgasms of my life, and now I just wanted to wrap her up in my arms and apologize over and over until she believed me.

"I am!" she shouted. "I *am* unreliable. I always let people down. Every single friendship and relationship and job I've managed to fuck up because I'm different from everyone else."

"You fit in here," I said more softly. "We're all different here. Maybe you just needed a little more magic in your life."

She pressed her lips together and the tears fell faster. "At least this time it wasn't my fault that everything fell apart." She wiped her eyes and wandered to the bedroom door, holding it open for me to pass. "You can let yourself out."

And my world shattered as I turned toward the door.

27
HARLOW

I'd thought about leaving several times that night and many times after. I'd wanted to storm out into the darkness and catch the first bus to anywhere but Maple Hollow. I would have if it wasn't for a second wave of illness hitting Willow that morning. I couldn't bring myself to abandon her. But I'd promised myself that as soon as she wasn't going through a box of tissues a day, I was out of there. Until then, I had a strict "No Jordyn" policy.

Jordyn had tried to come into the café a few times, but Wyatt had told her off before she could get to the front door. He kept vigil at the table beside the front door and I paid him in copious coffees. He was giving up his sleeping time, but he insisted on staying to help however he could while Willow was condemned to her bed. And right then, helping meant protecting my heart from the girl who'd broken it.

How could I have been such a fool? There was no way a girl like Jordyn would've fallen for me. She had just been using me to fix a summoning mistake.

Jordyn had finally gotten the point after Wyatt had

gotten Billy involved. I'd fought back the twinge of guilt when both men had scolded her. I couldn't believe even Billy was on my side.

On the third night since our breakup—God, was it even a breakup?—I was rage-cleaning again.

I'd dated girls for months, years, and it hadn't come close to the way I was feeling now. We'd only slept together once, had shared only a handful of dates and stolen kisses, and still, it had just felt so right. She was the other half of the same coin—balanced in the ways I was chaotic, timid in the ways I was bold, serious in the ways I was sarcastic.

I groaned and threw the dish towel into the bucket of dirty mugs. Why did the sex have to be explosive? We'd barely even scratched the surface. I bet she had a million more tricks up her sleeve. What kind of magic could she bring into the bedroom? Great, now I was torturing myself thinking about her. The ghost of her ex-girlfriend had been there for every moment, every shared kiss, whispering in her ear and saying God knew what, and she hadn't told me.

Had any of it been her choice? Or had she been shoved into every interaction we'd shared? Had she even wanted to be with me? The look in her eyes when I'd told her to leave made me think yes... but that didn't excuse her lies. I couldn't trust her.

The front doorbell clanged, and I frowned down at the table I was cleaning. I'd forgotten to lock the door.

"We're closed," I grumbled without looking up.

"Sorry for the interruption." A saccharine-sweet voice met my senses along with the smell of fish and . . . alcohol?

I lifted my head to see Katie standing a few steps into the café. She clutched a small container in her gloved hands, but her appearance surprised me more than anything. Her hair was pulled back with a baseball cap atop it, but the skin around her neckline looked tight and irritated. Her white overalls were covered in smudges of blood, mud, and dried fish bits. Did fishmongers actually work at this time of night? It seemed like a morning thing.

But it was the look in her eyes that sent ice through my veins.

"It's been a long night, Katie," I said warily. "Any chance we can talk in the morning?"

"Oh, sorry," she said in her too-high voice. "I just wondered if you wanted these?" She offered the Tupperware to me and held my gaze. Her makeup was much heavier than usual and caked around the small lines near her mouth, nose, and eyes. I hadn't asked how old she was, but I'd assumed she was around my sister's age.

I took it from her and sniffed it. "What is this?"

"Salmon," she said. "I noticed you were starting to add bagels to your menu and I thought you might want to try to add some lox to them? If you enjoy them, maybe we could work out an arrangement? I'm an excellent fish supplier, just ask Billy Bacchus."

"Thanks," I gritted out, turning and putting the fish in the mini fridge of milks behind me. "But I think Willow will need to give approval for any menu changes." I added in a faux whisper, "I've learned that lesson the hard way."

"Of course, take your time." She tittered a high laugh. "But maybe I can make you a sample really quick? Then you can really sell it to Willow?" She gave me a wink that looked almost painful.

"I'm not really into fish. Sorry." Not a complete lie, but something inside of me was telling me to decline her offer.

"It's an acquired taste, right?" The question sounded more like an accusation. "Sometimes it takes a new preparation to turn you on to something. Funny enough, I used to hate nutmeg, but now I can't get enough of it."

"Sure."

"A little cream cheese, chives, and pepper totally changes the taste of smoked salmon. I can show you." She cocked her head and watched me a little closer than before.

I took a step back into the entryway of the kitchen. "Maybe another time. I have a bit of a stomachache. Maybe I'm catching what Willow has. Been feeling a bit . . . off."

"That's too bad. If there's anything you or Willow need, let me know. Okay?"

"Thanks, Katie. That's really nice of you. But really, I just need to get some sleep. See you around?" I waited for her to get the hint and walk away, but her feet stayed planted.

"Oh sure," she said, ignoring yet another hint to leave. "I just figured us humans have got to stick together. We're all we've got in this town, after all."

I arched a brow at her. "What do you mean by that?"

"It's sad, really," she said, waving her hand in a dismissive motion. "Not everyone thinks we belong here. That we shouldn't be consorting with the paranormal."

"That's ridiculous. Willow fits in here. Everyone loves her." That sinking feeling in my stomach was turning into a crater.

"But it's not like we belong here. Don't you agree?" She stalked closer, but my stunned limbs wouldn't move. "It's nature. Humans should date humans, and monsters should date monsters, you know?"

"I haven't heard anyone else saying that."

Her eerie green eyes pierced mine, the look in her gaze ringing with a familiarity that made the hairs on the back of my neck stand on end.

"Then you're not listening," she said breezily, her work

boots trailing after me on the other side of the counter. "Did you know that a lot of people were really unhappy when Lou and Jordyn started dating? Why Jordyn would choose to be with a human—even if she was part demon—is beyond me." Those intense eyes shot to me. "And why she'd choose one a second time is even more baffling."

Lou was half demon? Had Jordyn told me that? I guessed it didn't matter anymore.

"Katie, have you been drinking?" I asked.

She flourished her fingers at me. "I have to wash my hands with rubbing alcohol unfortunately." She cackled. "It's the only thing that gets the fish stink out. Terrible for the skin. People always think I've been boozing it up all night, but no. It's just to deal with the fish smell."

"Okay . . ." I edged toward the rack of knives behind me. Something felt wrong. Really, really wrong. "I think it's time for you to leave. Maybe we can talk about this some other time . . . with witnesses."

She threw her head back in laughter, a high-pitched sound that held no humor and sent panic into my chest. "You're so funny, Harlow!"

When she finally met my eyes again, she became a thing of nightmares. A lock of hair escaped from her under her baseball cap, except that it wasn't hair at all—it was a strand of seaweed. The cracks in her skin began peeling away at the corners of her eyes and mouth.

All at once, I remembered where I'd seen those green eyes. I saw it plainly now . . .

And they weren't human at all.

28

JORDYN

I slumped on the apothecary chair, immobilized by grief. I couldn't eat, couldn't sleep, couldn't move. I'd done some bad things before in my life, but I'd royally fucked this one up. It shouldn't hurt this bad. Harlow had been a stranger only a week ago . . . and yet everything inside of me felt hollow, lifeless, and broken.

Iris had taken over the customer service side of things for the last few nights while I'd rung people up in my nearly comatose state. Unfortunately, there were no elixirs on the shelf that fixed a broken heart—although there were some that would've helped numb the pain, but Iris refused to let me have them.

Lou sat cross-legged under the center table giving Ichabod scratches and it reminded me of the day I'd met Harlow, and my eyes misted with tears all over again. Goddess, I felt pathetic.

The apothecary hit a momentary lull, and Iris turned to me. "Finish your sandwich." She pointed at the pile of breadcrumbs I'd picked at and the glass she'd set beside me three hours ago. Iris was determined to mother me through the heartbreak. I didn't know what hydration had to do with a broken heart, but it seemed to be the hill she was willing to die on.

I picked up the glass and took a small sip.

The door opened and Rudy walked in, waving to a gaggle of tourists who were chasing him and snapping photos like paparazzi. His pumpkin head was certainly a crowd favorite. I didn't know what lies the humans needed to tell themselves to make Rudy make sense, but they all staunchly believed he was just a man in an elaborate costume. If they knew his head was really a pumpkin, they'd probably all go running for the hills, yet here they were, shoving their kids in front of him to get a photo for their socials.

"The two of you owe me an explanation," Rudy said by way of greeting. He held up the file on Lou's autopsy.

Iris crossed her arms and frowned at him. "We returned it the day after we borrowed it as promised."

Rudy's smug expression fixed on me as his hand rummaged around in his messenger bag. "The last page was missing. Normally, I'd have to report the two of you for tampering with local government documents." He held up a disheveled, stained piece of paper. "Luckily, I found it in the guttering by the gazebo."

"Rats," Iris muttered. "I worried there was still a page that got away in the wind."

I propped my elbows on the desk. "Sorry, Rudy." I could barely get the words out.

"Whoa," he said, turning his pumpkin head to me, "you look like you've been hit by a truck."

"It's a girl thing," Iris said out of the corner of her mouth.

I rolled my eyes. "Did that paper have anything of interest?" I gestured to the crumpled-up wad in his hand. "We already saw that the tox report didn't show any alcohol in her system."

Rudy pulled the edges of the paper apart and started smoothing it over the edge of the center table. "No alcohol. But this page shows saxitoxin in her system. My assistant failed to alert me to this particular toxin. Your intuition was right."

I stood a little too quickly and my eyes spotted. Damn, Iris probably was right. I should've drunk more water.

"Saxitoxin?" Iris asked. "What's that?"

"It's a paralytic toxin released by a pretty rare type of freshwater fish," Rudy said. "Did Lou have a penchant for exotic seafood?"

"No," Lou grumbled, climbing out from under the table where she'd been petting Ichabod.

Rudy reared back, color draining from his flesh. "Well, damn. Hi, Lou." He waved his spindly fingers. His hollow head twisted to Iris. "I'm guessing this is why you're investigating her death?"

"Yep," Iris said.

"I can't remember what I ate that day," Lou said. "It's all a blur, really."

"If you consumed this paralytic, that would make sense," Rudy replied. "It starts off with disorientation and dizziness before you go completely numb. That's probably why you ran off the road." He scratched the orange skin where a chin should have been. "So, no fish that day?"

"There were lox!" I practically shouted as I rounded the table. "Lou said someone was eating lox."

"Ah," Rudy said. "They could've substituted one for the other. It looks very similar to salmon."

"But who would have this weird kind of fish just lying around?" Iris asked.

Rudy shrugged. "Clearly, you've never been to a monster bash," he said with a chuckle that echoed around his head. "The swamp monsters love that stuff."

My heart skipped a beat. "Juniper," I whispered. Heat prickled across my skin. "Juniper was in the square the night of the scrying."

"Shit," Iris hissed.

We both bolted toward the door at the same time. Rudy whirled around as we passed him and looked as if he were debating following.

"Thank you, Rudy!" I shouted as we stumbled into the street and practically bowled over Agnes.

"Agnes!" I panted. "Have you seen Juniper? Do you know where she is?"

The vampire's shrewd red eyes narrowed. "Katie was just heading over to the café."

"But..." I looked at Iris and back to Agnes in confusion.

"Oh, you don't know?" Agnes asked with a surprised laugh. "You witches really aren't the brightest. How do you think she can sell her catches out of town if not as a human?"

29
HARLOW

Katie leaped over the counter with preternatural speed then grabbed a fistful of my shirt. I let out a garbled gasp instead of a scream, the air knocked out of me as she twisted me away from anything solid to hold on to before slamming me against the countertop. In her Katie form, she was shorter and smaller than me, but in her true form, Juniper was a head taller—and all muscle.

Shit. I should've grabbed a knife when I'd had the chance.

I fought back, clawing a hand down her face and peeling back clumps of sticky skin to reveal her wet, gray face underneath.

I gagged at the sight.

"You think you can have her, but you'll never make her happy," Katie—Juniper—seethed. Her voice had dropped two octaves from the sickly sweet one she'd put on before.

How had she so wildly changed?

"What are you talking about?" I reached to claw at her

219

again, but she grabbed my wrist and slammed it against the edge of the counter with a sickening crack. I let out a wail.

Where the fuck was Willow?

"Jordyn is meant to be with her own kind," Juniper hissed. "A paranormal."

"Dear God, tell me this isn't all because you're jealous?" I cried out as she twisted my wrist again. "This is insane!"

"We had a date planned. The same day Lou lost control of her roller skates and crashed straight into Jordyn. And Jordyn canceled our date the second she collided with that filthy, little human."

More seaweed dripped from her bandana. "Filthy? That's a little rich coming from a swamp monster, don't you think?"

Juniper hissed, black ink seeping from her teeth. "Even after Jordyn broke up with her, Lou didn't get the hint. I ran into her when I was selling fish two towns over, and she said she was missing home and planning on moving back here." She spat, and the black saliva sizzled through the countertop. "And I couldn't have that, could I?"

My stomach boiled over. I made a mental note to tell Willow it would've been nice to have had a heads-up that swamp monsters had acid spit.

"You killed Lou," I snarled. Not a question, but an accusation.

"I was *protecting* Jordyn!" she screeched. "I was taking care of her! Lou didn't know what it took to love a witch as powerful as Jordyn could be. Then I waited for months while Jordyn got her head on right. Dropping hints and care baskets. I was there to remind her that she was better than Lou. We were so close to rekindling a flame that would have rivaled hell itself. But then *you* rolled into town and took her away from me."

Her hand flew up to my throat, sharpened nails cutting through her gloves.

I managed to bark out a final "Willow!" before Juniper squeezed, cutting off my air supply. My face pinpricked with a thousand needles. Blood vessels burst in my eyes. My vision spotted.

"Your sister sampled my cuisine the other night," Juniper said with an evil grin. "I don't think she's going to be waking up for some time."

My heart plummeted to my boots. Did Juniper poison Willow because of me? All because I fell for a witch?

I kicked as hard as I could but made no contact. The expended energy made my muscles ache even more. My lips mouthed a plea, but it was no use. Juniper was going to murder me in the middle of my sister's café, then find Jordyn. All the fight I had in my body tried and failed to rally.

Tears sprang to my eyes. This was it. She was going to kill me.

The light started dwindling away when a blast sounded behind me. Glass sprayed through the air, and a force of energy sent Juniper stumbling back, giving me just enough leeway to take in a lungful of precious air.

"Juniper!" a familiar voice screamed. "Let her go!"

Juniper spun me around, her viselike grip returning to my throat as she held my back to her front like a human shield.

Jordyn stood in the doorway, her whole body vibrating as wind twisted around her and moonlight beamed from her eyes. The air filled with static, zaps of lightning flying around the room as a storm cloud of power loomed over Jordyn's head. She was a goddess of elements. My savior. If this was the last thing I'd see before I died, I was glad it was her.

Iris appeared a few steps behind Jordyn, all charged up with magic and ready to release havoc with her coven mate. Agnes and Rudy stood a few steps beyond, their faces slack with shock.

"Stop this, Juniper," Jordyn growled. "Let her go or I swear hurting her will be the last thing you do."

"You couldn't just stay away from another human, could you, Jordyn?" Juniper seethed. "You flaunted her in front of me just to hurt me—"

"No," Jordyn cut in.

"You brought her to *my swamp!*" Juniper screamed and squeezed my throat tighter.

My eyes bugged.

A bolt of lightning landed just beside us, and I jolted, a silent scream forming on my lips.

"Can't hit me without hitting her, love," Juniper said. "I'm fixing this for us. You and me, Jordyn. We can finally be together without the humans in the way."

Agnes stepped forward. "This is enough, Juni," she hissed coldly. "You've taken this hate of humans too far."

Of all the people I thought would come to my defense, I certainly didn't think it would be the vampire.

"This is what you wanted, Agnes," Juniper crowed. "No more humans living amongst the monsters."

Jordyn let out a sound so feral, I wondered if she was part wolf. "Even if you were the last being in town, I would never choose someone as hateful as you, Juniper. Never."

Juniper froze for a second, and I was sure Jordyn's words had landed heavier than a bolt of lightning ever could. Still, Juniper said, "You just don't see it yet, love. You'll see one day. You and I were always meant to be together."

Something slimy and bitter filled my mouth, clammy fingers shoving it down my throat and forcing me to swallow.

"No!" Jordyn's scream filled my ears.

Iris gaped at her. "You've lost your fucking mind."

More locals gathered, all bearing witness to the display. But no one moved; no one could. Even with all the magic in Maple Hollow, who was faster than this swamp monster? No one seemed willing to risk an attack while I was in the crossfire.

Juniper tightened her grip and yanked me backward, edging us toward the hall that led to the back door. We skimmed the countertop by the knife block, and I knew this was my only chance. But when I reached for the knives, my broken wrist wouldn't lift. Sharp pain shot through me. My mouth bobbed open like a fish on dry land. My vision was narrowing, the periphery filling with black, and I desperately clung to consciousness.

Juniper let out a watery choking sound and her hand released me.

I dropped to my knees, sucking in sharp breaths of air. I looked up to find Juniper staring vacantly above me, the tip of a knife protruding from the center of her chest. She dropped like a stone, revealing a wild and terrifying Lou standing behind her.

A twisted grin pulled at Lou's lips. "Damn, that felt good."

I was holding on the best I could, but my eyes were drooping as sweet oxygen rushed into me and my heart pounded in my chest. The last thing I saw was Lou's eyes fixed on me as madness turned into calm. Then everything went black.

30
JORDYN

I sat slumped in the armchair beside Harlow's bed, reliving the last time we were here over and over again as I watched her sleep.

This was my fault. All of it.

Harlow was bright and vibrant and loving, and I'd dragged her into this danger. First, it had been because I'd wanted to get rid of Lou, but quickly—faster than I'd like to admit—I'd kept her close because I was falling for her. Because she looked at me like I was something more than just a product of my town. Because she and I seemed to see each other in ways no one else ever had.

And it had felt so good and right to be loved by her that I'd never considered pulling her into this Lou investigation would lead to this.

Harlow here, *hurt*, because of me.

The café had been shut for repairs . . . and lack of staff, considering Juniper had poisoned both Miller sisters. Wyatt had become an absolute watchdog. I could hear him doting upon Willow upstairs even as I held vigil beside Harlow's bed. The werewolf refused to let Willow get out of bed for anything, and I knew for certain what she was to him—far more than just a friend or even a crush. It was so much clearer now that Willow was injured.

It turned out that Willow had ingested a small amount of the poisoned fish—the same one that had killed Lou. I assumed that had been intentional on Juniper's part. When Willow had been given a strong antidote, it had only taken her a few hours to start demanding Wyatt give her some space again.

Willow was more stubborn than any human woman I knew, and Wyatt was doing his damnedest to take the brunt of it. If only he'd tell her that he couldn't just leave her, especially so close to the full moon.

But Harlow...

Harlow had slept for the last twenty-four hours, and I hadn't moved from the chair since.

A light rap on the bedroom door sounded, and Iris peeked her head inside. "Any changes?"

I shook my head, my heart cracking all over again. This was my fault, my responsibility.

"She rolled over before," I croaked, my voice shredded from lack of sleep and tears.

Iris tried to feign a smile. "That's promising." There wasn't much conviction in her tone. She opened the door and placed a small glass vial beside Harlow's bed. "Healing tonic. I tried a new recipe. Maybe this one will help revive her."

I scrubbed a hand down my face. "Or maybe that poison will keep her asleep until she withers away."

Our magic wasn't working. Never in my life had I felt so helpless. I was so desperate, I'd even called in a human doctor to help, but she'd just said it was a waiting game.

Iris nudged me to get up. "Let me sit with her for a little while."

I didn't budge. "I don't want to leave her. Not until she wakes."

"When's the last time you peed?" Iris put her hands on her hips. "You're asking for a UTI, you know that?"

I let out a half-hearted laugh. "I don't need you mothering me right now."

"Of course you do," Iris said, tugging me to a stand. I didn't have the energy to fight her. "Besides, I think there's someone else who needs you right now."

I looked up to see Lou peeking her head in. My shoulders drooped as I sighed. "Okay, fine. Two minutes and I'm coming right back. Call me if she moves."

Iris saluted me. "Will do."

I followed Lou to the front of the café, where half the town had set to work fixing the damage. It was a sight to see. Billy was painting the trim. Agnes was repairing the witch's broom coatrack. Dougall was tightening the screws on the barstools. Even Rudy and his wife were decorating the windows with the pumpkins Harlow and I had picked only a few days earlier.

My heart twinged anew. It was beautiful seeing the town come together like this. Despite this supposed alliance, despite the friction between the paranormal and human, Willow and Harlow were ours. They belonged to us —to Maple Hollow—and we would get Witch's Brew Café back to its former glory in no time.

A dozen heads turned toward me as I wandered out.

"Anything?" Billy asked hopefully. The group muttered their agreement.

I shook my head. "Not yet."

They all looked a little deflated at that but turned their energy back to their work.

"I'm just saying goodbye to this one." I hooked my thumb at Lou, and everyone whined and grumbled. Lou was visible to everyone now, and she offered them a sad, little smile at their protestations.

"Do you have to go, Lou?" Rudy asked. "It's been kind of nice having you around again."

"Yeah," Billy added. "I know Maple Hollow could sure use a resident ghoul if you're interested in the job."

"Sorry, Billy," she said. "It's time for me to move on."

He nodded. "We'll miss you, kid."

She gave him a wink. "I'll see you on the other side."

The group bade her farewell, and I walked her out onto the square, wanting a final goodbye, just the two of us. When we were sure we'd walked out of earshot, we let out matching sighs.

"It's been an adventure," I said.

"It sure has." She hugged me, her body corporeal but devoid of warmth.

I squeezed her tight and dropped my head onto her shoulder. I didn't think I'd ever get a chance to hug her again.

"I'm so sorry, Lou," I murmured. "For everything."

She gave me one final squeeze and pulled away. "Don't you dare be sorry. Juniper wouldn't have stopped with me— or Harlow, for that matter. I'll actually be able to rest now that I know how and why I died. Thank you for giving me that peace."

That stinging reminder hitched in my throat. I wiped away my tears and nodded.

Lou flashed me a bittersweet smile. "And we had a little bit of fun too, right?"

I mustered a weak smile to mirror hers. "I guess there was some fun."

"I'm so proud of you for realizing what you want . . . and even being willing to kill to keep it," she added with a morbid chuckle. "Don't get me wrong, the old Jordyn was great. But the new Jordyn is amazing."

"Thank you." It didn't feel like a big enough gesture of appreciation, but the knot in my throat was growing with every passing second.

"Goodbye, Jordyn," she said, lifting a hand as her visage flickered. "And do me a favor?"

"Anything," I squeaked.

"Tell Harlow to take care of you too." Lou's distant voice was fading fast. "She's a good one. Hang on to her."

Another river of tears slid down my cheeks as I nodded. I waved as she fractured into bright, warm lights then drifted away like sparks of a campfire floating into the night sky.

I stared at the spot where she'd disappeared. I would always miss her. In life and death, she'd taught me more about myself than anyone else could . . . except, perhaps, for the beautiful woman lying unconscious in the café because of me.

I felt equally guilty and grateful that Lou and I had had this time together—one last story between the two of us to share for eternity. We finally got the ending we both deserved. Whatever the afterlife held for Lou, I hoped it was beautiful and peaceful and filled with the slightest bit of mischief I knew she loved.

The café door opened behind me, and Iris shouted, "She's waking up!"

31
HARLOW

I didn't know if it was dawn or dusk or how many hours had ticked by since I'd passed out. I sucked in a sharp breath as it all came flooding back to me: Jordyn, Lou, Katie, Juniper . . .

As I blinked the world back into focus, a weight pressed into the mattress and I saw Jordyn perched on the bed beside me, holding my hand in hers.

Her eyes were so watery, I could barely make out her pupils. "Hi," she said, her voice breaking.

"Hi," I whispered back. I rubbed a hand across my neck. I expected it to be bruised and swollen, but I couldn't feel any injuries. "Juniper?"

"Dead." Jordyn hung her head. "I should've known it was her. She'd always been a bit weird about my relationship with Lou, but murder? I didn't think she was capable of that." She wiped a knuckle under her eye. "I'm so sorry, baby. I should've known. I should've protected you."

I shook my head, unable to find the words, and then I

remembered. "Willow?" I practically leaped out of bed, and Jordyn had to grab me by the shoulders and gently steer me back against my pillow.

"She's okay. She's okay," Jordyn reassured me, holding me down with a tentative firmness until the words sank in and I stopped battling her. "She woke up last night."

"How long have I been out?"

"A whole day," she said. "Nearly taken out by Juniper's surprise pocket fish."

"Her what?" My stomach roiled but I pushed on. "Never mind. Willow's really okay? Where is she?"

Jordyn's hand found mine again. "She's resting in bed upstairs." She placed a kiss on the back of my hand. "Iris went to check on her and said she's back to her normal spirits again but that Wyatt won't let her leave her room until he can't scent the poison in her system anymore."

"Good man," I said with an approving nod.

"From what I've heard, he's likely exaggerating about how much he can still smell." Jordyn gave a weak laugh. "Iris told me that the toxin was likely out of her system hours after Juniper died. I know I should have checked myself, but I haven't left this room since I carried you into it . . . well, except for two minutes."

I balked. "You've been in here the entire time?"

She swept a strand of hair off my face. "I didn't want you to be alone when you woke up."

I lifted my other hand and rolled my wrist. The muscles were stiff, but it didn't hurt to move it. I looked at Jordyn. "How?"

Her cheeks dimpled. "Sometimes it pays to have a witch as a girlfriend."

She'd fixed my broken wrist with her magic alone?

She cleared her throat. "That is . . . if I am your girl-friend? If I can be your girlfriend still?"

"I . . ." I took a deep breath.

What was I supposed to say? This was all so much. Before Juniper's attack, I was planning on leaving town and moving on to the next job, next town, next relationship. That was what I did. I messed up one thing and moved on to the next.

I looked around the room. "Where's Lou?"

"She's moved on. Permanently this time," Jordyn said, rhythmically rubbing her thumb across the back of my hand. I knew she was nervous. I'd not so subtly dodged that girlfriend question. "The last thing she said to me was to hang on to you." She let out a defeated huff. "But I don't think she realized how badly I fucked this up before it really even began."

I hummed, not wanting to confirm or deny. Regardless of whether Lou was still here or not, Jordyn had lied to me about her. And knowing that the ghost of her ex-girlfriend had been watching *might* have changed my perspective on a few of our first encounters.

Jordyn looked at me with those pleading kaleidoscope eyes. "Say something."

I let out a long breath, buying myself some time, before finally saying, "I think . . . I need some time to think." I care-fully extracted my hand from hers.

I hated the hurt etched all over her face. Hated that I was the one who put it there. But I couldn't ignore the hell I'd been put through since meeting her. Except when she wet her lips and looked at me like she was now.

"I was nearly *murdered.* Willow was poisoned. The café is a mess. And the ghost of your ex-girlfriend threw me against a wall while I was still *naked* after we hooked up. And it's just . . . a lot."

She didn't say anything for a long moment.

"When you say it like that, I suppose it *is* a lot. And even without all that drama, I'm a lot. My life is a lot. But just know that I'm here and . . ." She leaned in and pressed a final kiss to my temple. "I want to be with you," she whispered against my skin, sending ripples of goose bumps dancing down my spine. "And I will wait for you to decide, however long you need, but just know that my heart is right here with you."

My eyes welled.

Jordyn stood, the flimsy mattress wobbling without her added weight. "I'm going to go help with the cleanup," she said, trying to pretend that she hadn't just bared a little piece of her soul to me. "Do you need anything? Food? Water?"

I smiled sadly. "A pumpkin-spice chai would be nice."

She narrowed her eyes at me and shook a finger. "Only if you promise to drink a whole glass of water first."

"Done," I said.

"And I'm bringing you a muffin, too," she added over her shoulder.

The drink request seemed to reignite her spirits. I hadn't told her goodbye or that I didn't want to be with her, just that I needed some time and space to think. Clearly, she was going to seize the opportunity to sway my opinion however she could.

I pressed my lips together, watching her until she closed the bedroom door.

Did I really want to get into a full-blown relationship with a witch? In a paranormal town where a monster had tried to *end* me? But if ever there was a girl wild enough to tame my heart, it would be a witch. And if ever there was a town that could contain my wandering chaos, maybe Maple Hollow was it...

And maybe Jordyn was worth it.

32
JORDYN

I stocked the vials in neat rows while Iris explained the benefits of different headache elixirs to one of the town werewolves. The shop had quieted down considerably since Halloween had come and gone. No more tourists being delighted by the potions and displays. No more posing for selfies and wondering if people were "just looking." No more spooky music playing over and over on a track to "add to the ambience," as Billy put it. Now, it was just locals coming in for their usual remedies.

We would have a few weeks' reprieve before the novelty of a Halloween-themed town started pulling drips and drabs of people in again in the new year. We needed the tourism and revenue, but it was nice to have a break.

I heard Ichabod's little mewls, and I turned to find him purring away under the table. I bent down to peek and found none other than Harlow sat there, giving him a scratch.

My mouth fell open.

I had been actively avoiding the café, giving Harlow

space to figure out what she wanted with me—if anything at all. My heart had sunk a little more with each day I hadn't seen her. I was beginning to wonder if maybe it really was over. But here she was, under the apothecary table as if summoned by my hopes alone.

When Harlow spotted me, she jolted, banging her head on the table. "Oh, hey," she said as if I were the one in a surprising place. She rubbed the top of her head. "Iris said you weren't working today."

I arched my brow at Iris, who just gave me a grin and put a finger to the side of her nose. I rolled my eyes. Of course she was meddling.

Harlow sheepishly climbed out, Ichabod pawing at her legs. She finally relented and picked him up for more scratches.

"So you've been secretly coming here to pet my cat?" I asked with a half smile. "Why doesn't that surprise me?"

"Little tattletale." Harlow kissed the top of Ichabod's head. "His purring gave me away. Thank goodness for that. I feel like a bit of a jerk for avoiding you, but I wanted to know how you were doing and, uh, Iris was keeping me updated."

I looked her up and down. "From now on, ask me, not Iris."

"Okay," she hedged.

"Okay," I echoed awkwardly. "It's, um, really nice to see you."

She'd trimmed her hair again; her bangs were shorter. Luna, the local stylist, had done a good job with the cut— very wolfish. Harlow fit right in.

"You look . . . well. Really well."

Fuck me and all the moons and stars. I needed to stop talking.

These weren't the things I wanted to say. I didn't want

to just tell her she looked well like a fool. I wanted to ask her real questions. Like if she'd thought about us or if she missed me as much as I missed her. Like if it felt like a part of her had been missing since that night at the café. Like maybe the things we were feeling were a whole hell of a lot closer to love than we'd first thought. I was dying to hear if she would give us another try.

Instead, I swung my arms back and forth, waiting for her to break the awkward silence.

"Thanks," she finally said, saving us.

Goddess, I wanted to kiss her so badly. I wanted to feel her arms wrapped around me. I wanted to tell her all of the sacred, little words that had been screaming in my mind from the moment I saw Juniper's hand around her throat—the ones I'd been terrified I might not get a chance to say.

"Uh, well, I should be going." Harlow gave Ichabod one final kiss on the top of his head and set him back down. "Willow's taken the day off so I'm shutting things down myself."

I smiled at the pride that laced her words.

That was a big deal. A really big deal. For both Willow and Harlow.

I wanted to hug Harlow and tell her how proud I was of her. I knew how hard it was for her to stick things out. Once she messed up, she preferred fleeing to learning. But here she was, helping run the café, developing her skills, and gaining her sister's trust. She'd chosen to stay. Maybe she'd be willing to move on from the mess I'd made too?

But instead of sharing these thoughts, I just said, "Okay, well, have a good night."

What the fuck is wrong with me? I silently screamed at myself.

She was *finally* here, the girl I'd been dreaming of seeing

239

for the last several weeks, and all I could say to her was "have a good night"?

Ugh. Goddess, let me whither into dust right now.

"Okay, bye," Harlow said, and I could tell she was a little disappointed in my response.

She stooped to give Ichabod one more scratch before she turned to leave. But not before giving Iris a little wave as she went.

Ask her to stay! Ask her on a date! Grab her and kiss her! Something! But no words would come. I was terrified. Paralyzed to the spot.

Iris farewelled the werewolves with a baggy of new potions and then zeroed in on me, annoyance wrinkling her forehead the moment the customers had passed me.

"What are you doing?" she hissed, her green eyes boring into me.

"What do you mean, what am I doing?"

"She was right *here!*" Iris pointed to the spot where Harlow had just stood. "She was right in front of you, giving you the big heart eyes! The girl you've been *pining* over."

I folded my arms across my chest. "I haven't been pining."

"Oh, really?" Iris guffawed. "Is that why you're drinking a bottle of wine and watching rom-coms every night? Is that why you stand at the living room window and peek down the back alley to where the café dumpsters are, hoping to get a glimpse of her? Have your eyes just been extra watery the past few weeks? Cutting lots of onions? And we just so happen to be running low on tissues constantly?"

Exasperated, I threw my hands up. "Okay, well, what was I supposed to say?"

She scoffed. "Literally everything. Everything you feel in your heart." She pointed at the door. "Go!"

"Go where?"

"Go to the café and tell her that you miss her," Iris said. "Tell her all the things you've been drowning in wine the last few weeks. Tell her what's going on in here." She poked me in the sternum.

"Ouch." I groaned. "Seriously, Iris."

"You're going to lose her, Jordyn. You're going to miss your chance to make this right. You let things fall apart with Lou because you were scared, and let's be honest. It was never right between you two. But this is so right! Don't live the rest of your life with more regrets."

Her words stung, and I knew by the set of her mouth and the tightness in her gaze that she felt a modicum of guilt for being so harsh.

But I also needed the verbal slap in the face. I'd thought I was giving Harlow some space to figure things out, but maybe I'd been avoiding her a little too. Maybe I'd dismissed her when she needed me to be the one to make the first move—without a ghost shoving us into a kiss.

I rolled my shoulders back and shook out my arms like I was about to enter a boxing ring. "Okay." I couldn't live with myself if I never told her how I truly felt.

"Okay? Yes!" Iris cheered, opening the door and windmilling her arm to usher me out. "Don't come back without a girlfriend."

My stomach twisted in knots as I stared down the row of buildings to the café. An unceremonious shove from Iris got my feet moving.

Goddess, help me.

33
HARLOW

I hummed to myself as I stacked the fresh dishes under the food cabinet, ready for the next day. I tried to distract myself from that interaction in the apothecary but couldn't. God, Jordyn had smelled exactly the same—witchy, earthy, sweet, and spicy. My stomach somersaulted just remembering it. Was it weird that I was smelling her? I'd wanted to tell her that I'd missed her, but then everything had been so awkward and I'd started worrying I'd waited too long.

Was she mad? Was she over me? Was this thing between us done before we gave it a fair chance?

A knock at the front door made me startle, and I let out a little muttered curse. I bet it was Willow checking on me. She was supposed to be getting a massage at Witching Hour Wellness, relaxing for the first time in ages, but I wouldn't put it past her to come check on me anyway.

I unlocked the door and opened it, ready with a witty retort on the tip of my tongue. But when I opened the door, it wasn't Willow waiting there.

Jordyn stood, arms wrapped around herself, shivering against the late-autumn wind. Her red cheeks were chapped, and steam whorled from her mouth, but her eyes pinned me with hopeful determination.

I opened my mouth to offer another awkward hello, but she was already moving. She grabbed me by the back of the neck and pulled me into a kiss.

My hands lifted instantly, hauling her into me and across the threshold. I kicked the door closed and pinned her against it, fervently kissing her with all the pent-up yearning that had been building over the weeks we'd been apart.

Lightning zipped under my skin with the feel of her hot mouth on mine. I sucked her bottom lip between my teeth, pulling a moan from her lips. My hands dipped under her sweater, across the smooth planes of her stomach, and up to cup her breasts.

"Wait," she murmured against my mouth, and I pulled back.

Right. Maybe a sex frenzy wasn't the best thing right this second.

"Keep thinking what you're thinking." She panted. "But I need to tell you something first."

She wrapped her arms around my waist and pulled me against her as if she needed every part of us to touch. I rested my forehead against hers, loving the way our warm breaths coalesced.

"I know we've been through a lot in a short amount of time," she whispered. "And I know you have every reason not to trust me, but I promise you, Harlow, I swear on my magic and the Moon Goddess and this burning feeling in my chest, I swear I will never, ever lie to you again."

Those rich hazel eyes lifted to meet mine, so close our

noses nearly touched. I wanted to bridge the distance, but she pulled her head back to look deep into my eyes.

"And I know it's too early to say this, but I have to. I don't want to live wishing I'd told you." Her eyes blazed, sending something like terror and excitement into my veins.

I sucked in a sharp breath, waiting for whatever it was she thought was more important than taking off our clothes and commencing our reunion in the best way I could imagine.

"I love you," she said, and my whole world shattered and fused back together anew. "With every ounce of my soul, I love you."

My hands bracketed her face, and I pulled her into another kiss. My heart was exploding in my chest, my stomach doing flips, and fireworks lighting up my soul as I broke our kiss for just long enough to say, "I love you too."

She smiled against my lips.

I scooped at the backs of her knees and pulled her up. Tender legs wrapped around my waist as I walked us toward my room. We were going to make up for all the time we'd lost being apart.

Her fingers raced through my hair, but once the door shut, they eagerly pulled at my shirt buttons. I laid her down on the bed and pulled her sweater over her head. Her long mahogany locks flowed down her bare chest, making my mouth water.

Fuck, she was more beautiful than I remembered.

In a blink, our clothes lay in a pile on the floor and she was pulling at my wrists until I was lying beside her. My thighs spread for her as my back hit the soft sheets and two eager fingers found my throbbing center. A hungry moan left my lips as our eyes met.

"I missed you so much," she breathed, the heat of lust in her eyes igniting an inferno low in my belly.

"Show me," I taunted.

A wickedly sultry smile tipped her lips before she lowered herself until her head was at the place where her fingers were already building my pleasure. She alternated between sucking and rolling her tongue over my needy nerves, the desperation and relief I felt knowing that she was really here taking me higher, faster. I couldn't believe this was real. Jordyn was between my legs, unraveling sweet pleasure within me until I could feel the rising orgasm fill my chest and overflow into my limbs. Every muscle in my core tightened until two fingers plunged deep inside of me. One moment, my head was swimming in the heat of the moment, and the next, every nerve ending was awoken with electricity.

Images of the night she'd saved me flashed behind my tightly closed eyelids. Her magic filled the room like it had then, the static charge and overwhelming buzz bringing me crashing into a climax bigger than life itself.

"Holy fuck, Jordyn."

Her touch had been addicting before, but this . . . this was something new. How could I possibly ever live without this every chance we got?

Jordyn kissed up my stomach, breasts, and neck until our lips finally met. Her sweet kiss was still glossed with my release. I needed this woman more than air or sunlight or the ruined and repaired heart in my chest. Maybe I should become nocturnal like other residents of Maple Hollow just so this little witch and I could spend our days tangled up in sheets.

My hands moved up and down her body to memorize

each curve. The small dimples on her lower back were a precise fit for my fingertips. Her breasts fit perfectly in my cupped hands. The slope of her neck to her jaw was just the right angle for my palm to bring our kiss deeper.

Through the haze of utter love drunkenness, all I could hear was our tandem breathing. The world outside was calm and slow. I'd decided that staying in this little monster town was worth a real shot. I'd thought falling for the first person I'd met here had been a bad omen, but now I knew it was fate.

Fate.

God, maybe I believed in that too now. It wasn't too wild to believe with a girlfriend who could literally shoot pure energy from her hands and make me come so hard, I swore I heard angels singing.

What else could Jordyn make me believe in with another tangle around the sheets?

"What are you thinking about?" she asked between soft kisses.

I pulled at her hips, wanting to feel every inch of her that I could. "I'm thinking about how tired we're going to be tomorrow. And the next day . . . and the day after that."

She smiled, making every future yawn worth it. "As long as that's the only thing you'll regret in the morning, I'm fine with it."

I nodded. "Not having you riding my face for the next hour would be the only tragic thing to come from tonight."

Her eyes crinkled with a surprised laugh. "Ambitious tonight."

"We've taken it pretty slow. I mean, I don't even know what names you have picked out for our future kids yet. We have a lot of ground to cover."

That earned me a full belly laugh and a poke to the ribs. "Should I book the U-Haul?"

Our playful giggles ebbed into slow kisses once again.

"I love you, Harlow." Jordyn hummed, snuggling into me.

"I love you too, little witch."

34
JORDYN
ONE YEAR LATER

I stood nervously in the center of the gazebo, bouncing on my toes. The ground was slick with ice, another inch of snow having fallen the night before. Our spooky town was now blanketed in white. The details of city hall and the shops gave off a more festive than spooky vibe. Add a few string lights and evergreen trees and we'd practically be one of those Christmas towns. My desire to return to the black and grays of the town was tempered by Harlow's excitement for Christmas and eagerness to go frolic in the snow. I swore more and more every day that she was turning into a werewolf.

In a lineup of humans and paranormal, Harlow would be picked on our team every time.

"You're going to wear a hole in the floor doing that," Iris muttered beside me. "Calm down before Billy makes us repaint it."

"I can't calm down." I checked my watch for the hundredth time. "They should be here by now. Willow said three. Willow's never late."

"Yeah, but Harlow is! She probably wanted to stay longer," Iris reassured me. "And Willow didn't have a good enough excuse for getting her back here without telling her why."

"I'm freezing my ass off here," Agnes hissed from behind one of the spindly maples in the square.

"You all don't need to be here!" I grumpily shouted back. "Why don't you all just go home?"

"We don't want to miss this," Rudy called gleefully from his hiding spot. "Besides, it's not that cold."

"Easy for you to say," Agnes spat. "You don't even have an ass."

I rolled my eyes and glanced nervously at Iris. "They're going to ruin this for me, aren't they?"

"It's going to be fine," she said in her calmest, most even tone. She reached into her pockets and started fishing around. "Do you want something for the nerves?"

I narrowed my eyes at her. "Why are you so chill?"

"I may have smoked some calming herbs before we came out here," she said with a giggle. "It's a new blend. We're going to be rich as thieves."

"I thought I told you, no dipping into the apothecary stash." I pointed at her. "And if you do, you have to share with me."

"Sorry!" she said with a laugh as she turned out empty pockets. "Next time!"

Dougall came running down the road, his arms wheeling as he hit a patch of black ice. "Their car is just turning off Misty Lane! I repeat: their car is turning off Misty Lane!" he shouted and then dove with a belly flop behind a snowbank. "Less than ten minutes to go."

"And that's our chief of police, ladies, gentlemen, fangs, and ghouls," I muttered.

A throat cleared behind us, and we whirled to find Ramona standing there. Her hands were clasped in front of her like a bouncer, a spotless black trench coat covering her normal uniform of a well-tailored suit.

"Ramona," Iris whisper-yelled, "if you're going to be here, you need to hide."

"I've come to collect on a debt," she said, arching her brow at Iris. "Time's up, witchling."

Iris gaped at her. "What are you talking about?"

"You agreed to a date," Ramona said with a feral grin. "Within a year. And I have given you much longer than that out of the sheer kindness of my heart."

"Can this please wait a couple minutes, please?" Iris hissed. "You can wait just a *tiny* bit longer."

"I am good at many things. Waiting isn't one of them." Ramona's smile just widened. "Give me a time and I'll go."

"This is ridiculous," Iris snarled, darting looks out to the road and back to me, but Ramona didn't budge. The demon stood as frozen as a statue, staring daggers into Iris that were from hate or, worse, *heat*. I couldn't tell.

"I can hear the car!" Dougall called from his hiding spot.

"*Iris*," I whined. This was too important for her to mess up for me!

"You have to go," Iris insisted, trying to shove Ramona, but she didn't budge. She didn't even rock back on her heels. "Goddess, are you made of stone?"

"Iris!" I snapped, doubling the pace of my bouncing. "This is kind of important. Just pick a time!"

"Okay, fine." The redhead threw her hands in the air. "You can pick me up at seven. We'll go eat at the new Italian place."

Ramona gave a wicked grin and winked. "Done."

I blinked, and then she was gone, disappearing into thin air.

"Delightful. A date with a demon." I shook my head. "What are your parents going to say? What is the *coven* going to say? Also, that's one hell of an age gap between you two—"

Iris elbowed me as a car pulled into the square. "Worry about that later." She dashed down the steps and hid behind the nearest holly bush. I heard a sneeze somewhere in the general vicinity and then a chorus of, "*Shush!*"

Great, the whole town was here to listen in.

I'd tried to shoo away the first group of onlookers, but the stubborn harpies had just floated around the square until they thought I wouldn't notice them crouching next to the old maple tree.

I gripped the ring box in my pocket tighter. My nerves were shot, but I had no doubt in my mind that I wanted this more than anything.

Sweet Goddess, please, please let her say yes.

35
HARLOW

"Why are you turning here?" I asked Willow as her car pulled into the town square instead of around the back of the café.

"I'm just dropping you off here," my sister said a little too breezily.

"Wh-why?" My question was cut off when I spotted the gazebo. The path leading up to it was lined with candles, a heavy sprinkling of salt covering the iced-over path. Black curtains hung from either side of it, and more candles covered the space. Twinkling lights were strung up in zigzags from the ceiling, and in the very center . . . stood Jordyn.

She wore a flowing black-velvet dress and black combat boots, her hair pinned up in curls. She shifted her weight back and forth as she stared at my foggy car window like she'd just seen a ghost.

"Oh my god," I whispered.

There was only one thing this could be. There was no mistaking it for anything else.

I gaped at my girlfriend through the fogged window. "Holy shit."

"Go!" Willow unbuckled my seatbelt and shoved my shoulder. "She's probably freezing. Don't make her wait in the cold."

"I can't believe you didn't warn me!" I hissed, looking back at Willow. "I could've worn a cuter outfit! Where's your sisterly loyalty? Traitor!"

"You look great," my sister encouraged. "Go on." She leaned over and gave me a quick, fierce hug. "I love you, Harlow."

I smiled at her even as I said, "I'm never going to let you live this down, you know?"

She huffed. "Yeah, I know."

I tried—and failed—to gracefully exit the car, my foot slipping on a patch of ice and forcing me to grip the car door for dear life. Willow offered me a guilty smile as I straightened and shut the car door. I walked tentatively down the aisle of candles, my heart thundering as Jordyn beamed at me.

When I climbed the steps to the gazebo, she said, "Hey," the word coming out all squeaky. Something about her being just as nervous as I was made me calm down a little. We couldn't both be panicking.

"Hey," I said, brushing a quick kiss to her glossy red lips. "Want to tell me *why* Iris is hiding in that bush?"

I heard a muttered curse and the bush rattled.

Jordyn and I chuckled.

"Harlow." Jordyn grabbed my hand. "You captured my heart from the moment I first laid eyes on you. Maybe it took a few ghosts and cups of pumpkin spice to get me to realize it." We both laughed again. "But deep down, I always knew. The moon drew me to you like the waves to the shore. A beautiful siren's song, one I tried to pretend I didn't hear at first."

Her eyes were fixed on my face, but mine were taking in this moment and committing it to memory. The way the snow hung from the tree branches contrasted with her dark hair and soft eyes.

"But I knew when I had the courage to listen that you were always meant to be mine," Jordyn continued, "as I was always meant to be yours. You are brave and funny and smart and full of life and adventure, and I want to spend the rest of my life by your side. You and me," she finished with a hopeful smile.

Dammit, now my eyes were pricking with tears.

The edges of Jordyn's lashes were hung with her own as she fished a ring box out of her pocket. She took a deep breath before dropping to one knee. The small green leather box was emblazoned with my initials in gold, and she opened it to reveal a giant emerald set in a ring of diamonds on a latticed silver band.

I gasped. I couldn't have picked a ring more perfect for myself if I'd tried.

My chest filled with all the love that we'd built in the last year. Had it really only been a year? It felt like a lifetime. And I wanted a million more.

"Harlow," Jordyn said, getting choked up, "will you marry me?"

A tear slid down my cheek, and I shifted on my feet. The nervous energy and happiness made it hard to find the words.

"I can't believe you're doing this right now in the middle of the square." I choked on a laugh, remembering our first official date and the millions of wishes for more time in the small hours of the morning.

She pursed her lips, a slight tremble in her hand while she held out the biggest gesture anyone could have ever given me.

I closed my eyes as I reached into the pocket of my puffer vest and pulled out my own ring box. The one I'd been carrying around for weeks, not sure what the right time or the right place would be or if I'd picked the right ring. The box had become a comfort blanket that I couldn't leave the house without.

But of course, Jordyn was the one who took the lead.

I dropped to one knee across from her and opened the box.

The ring was her grandmother's. She'd given it to me three months ago when I'd gone to ask her coven for their blessing. It was a silver band dotted with delicate pearls that led to a square-cut diamond in the center.

"Only if you marry me too."

Tears streamed down Jordyn's face even as she laughed and nodded. "Yes."

"Yes," I said at the same time.

I grabbed her and pulled her into a kiss, our mouths colliding and our tear-streaked cheeks pressing against each other.

A cacophony of cheers erupted around us, and I pulled back to see half the town leaping up from behind trees, shrubs, and snowbanks. My mouth fell open as I looked around the square. I'd been so nervous I hadn't seen all of them.

Willow shouted, "Let's go celebrate in the Witch's Brew!" And everyone cheered in hearty agreement. "A round of hot chocolate on me!"

Jordyn and I rose and slid the engagement rings onto each other's fingers.

"I love you," I said, pulling her into a tight hug.

"I love you too." She brushed a kiss on my lips. "Fiancée."

"I like the sound of that." I smiled against her mouth, my laughter interrupting our kisses. "Are you sure you didn't put a love spell on me? Because I love you more than I ever thought was possible. I love you like it's magic."

Jordyn shook her head and kissed me again. "You're more stubborn than my magic."

I tugged her close to my side, where she would always belong.

36
JORDYN
TEN MONTHS LATER

T onight was Halloween. Our town's most important traditions would be celebrated in the square for all eyes to see. But in the small temple at the edge of the haunted woods, I was marrying the woman of my dreams.

"It's almost time," Iris announced, her face tilted up to the glass ceiling. Her red locks had been whisked up into a nest of braids and curls, and the sigils of our coven stretched across her forehead in gold paint that looked like a crown.

We'd talked so many times as girls about officiating each other's weddings, but I'd never thought this day would come. Now that it was really happening, I knew my best friend would tie my and Harlow's bond extra tight.

"You look beautiful." My mother gripped my hand in hers, a quick squeeze before my grandmother pulled me in for a hug.

"Harlow is lovely," Grandma whispered. "You've found someone just as special as you, my darling. I think some

263

magic runs in her veins. There's a perfect spark of mischief to her."

I smiled through welling eyes. That was one of the highest compliments a coven elder could give.

All day, all I'd been able to think about were the beautiful little moments that Harlow had made into memories. Our first trip outside of Maple Hollow, or getting caught in a downpour when we'd been scavenging for mushrooms in the forest, or that time we'd gotten locked in this very moon temple all night long. Each time had ended with us making love in a new, forbidden place that had made us giggle every time we'd reminisced about it. With anyone else, these were passing incidents, but with Harlow, they were sacred adventures, the things we'd explored both within the world and within each other.

The moon was smiling down on us, not full yet but still heavy with light and energy. Our coven respected the moon and drew power from its blessings each month, but on All Hallows' Eve, the veil between the planes of the living and the dead was thinner than ever. The ancestors of our coven could bear witness to our union, which would solidify Harlow's place in my world. She was one of ours now.

Merging human and witch traditions wasn't difficult. Harlow embraced each practice and never questioned our superstitions—even when it meant blessing every doorway with cinnamon each month or placing stones in the garden to help the plants grow. And since Harlow would now be my wife, the townspeople could never question her residence in Maple Hollow again.

"Places, everyone." My mother guided us through the door of the blessing room and into the large, open ritual space.

Every member of our coven had gathered with their

hands clasped to create a large circle of blessing around the room. They rhythmically hummed in unison as we approached the small break of hands that led to a candle-lined aisle. Crystals and even more candles dotted the middle of the sacred space. My mother and grandmother each kissed my cheek before stepping back to join hands and complete the circle behind me.

Waiting just inside the line of salt was Iris. With misty eyes and a bright smile on her face, she took my hand and led me down the walk to our positions at the center. I took a deep breath and wrung my hands, the nerves finally catching up to me.

The glass doors on the other side of the room opened and Willow stepped through. Her pretty, knee-length purple dress hugged her hips and dipped low on her chest. I couldn't help my smile at seeing my soon-to-be sister-in-law dressed up in anything but her work clothes. She beamed at me then looked over her shoulder.

My heart pounded louder and louder as Harlow stepped into the candlelight. Her eyes locked on mine, and a hoard of butterflies took flight in my gut. She was perfect. Her linen pants and shirt gave her a soft, ethereal silhouette. She'd wanted to grow her hair so we could braid flowers at the crown of her head, and each one made her look like an otherworldly beauty—part god, part goddess, and entirely perfect.

Willow waited until a new round of humming from the coven started before she led Harlow up the aisle. Like before, members of the coven filled in the ring so it was complete. A thin veil of white energy flowed overhead, and I felt the familiar essence of those who had passed on come to witness our souls bonding.

I took Harlow's hands in mine. The warmth of her fingers anchored me in place.

"*Dilectus, junctus, ligatus,*" Iris said, and the coven repeated after her. "*Pro arca, pro sanguine, pro magicis.*"

A burst of tiny firefly-like lights danced in the air above us, a sign that our love was being blessed by those who had come before us.

"Harlow." Iris turned her attention to her. "Do you accept this bond and love from now until your spirit joins the ever after?"

"And so much longer," Harlow answered. My chest tightened with emotion.

"Good answer," Iris whispered. "Jordyn, do you accept this bond and love from now until your spirit joins the ever after?"

I fought back tears to answer, "Yes. A thousand times over, yes."

Harlow's grip tightened in mine.

"*Dea. Terra. Mater. Benedictiones,*" Iris chanted, and the surrounding voices joined for three rounds.

Iris wrapped our joined hands in a white satin scarf then held her hand over the bundle. Energy, light, and air whirled around us in a gentle embrace. The candles flickered and sent light dancing on the walls, casting the shadows of the people who'd raised and protected me. A powerful feeling of unity overtook me, and the tears I'd been holding back finally broke free. My gaze passed from one face to another until I met one that I didn't expect to see.

A translucent set of eyes held mine, and a joyful warmth flowed through my limbs. Lou's proud face appeared for a brief moment, giving me an approving nod, before joining the balls of energy floating around us. I tried to keep track of her glowing orb but quickly lost her in the fray as tears clouded my vision.

"By the coven, I pronounce you wife and wife!" Iris's voice rang out before the room erupted in celebration.

Harlow's arms wrapped around me, and I pulled her in for a deep, savoring kiss. With our bonding ceremony complete, the spirits returned to their plane, leaving the room in dim candlelight.

"We did it," I said between tears and kisses. "We're married."

"And I'd do it again, a thousand times over."

I nodded, wiping away my wife's tears with my thumb, then took her hand.

Wife. Sweet Goddess, the word felt so good.

Together, we walked toward the exit, the coven following us, and headed outside to where our closest friends were waiting for us by the bonfire. We partook in music, cake, and celebration until the early hours of the morning. And when the festivities finally came to an end, Harlow and I watched the sunrise from the gazebo, where we began the first day of the rest of our lives in our sleepy, magical town as wife and wife.

The End

Where to find us!

Ali K. Mulford

K. Elle Morrison

ACKNOWLEDGMENTS

From Ali K. Mulford

Thank you so much to all of my Patrons! I love writing new stories, commissioning spicy art, and getting to connect with you on Patreon! A very special thank you to Morgan, JC, Samantha, Abigail, Val, Lindsay, Bri, Kat, Stacy, Lauren, Latham, Leigh, Jaime, Kelly, Hannah, Sarah, Amy, Marissa, Ciara, Linda and Katie! Thank you for being on this bookish adventure with me!

From K. Elle Morrison

This book couldn't have happened without Caroline Acebo, Norma Gambini, and Holly Dunn. What a dream this process has been!

Thank you to my Patreon members who support my dreams, art addiction, and mini series.